"I wondered why you never got married. You're more'n pretty enough."

Eliza's cheeks grew warm. The cover of night coaxed words into the open. "There was one special someone once. But he just…disappeared."

"Man was a damned fool," Jonas said with enough conviction to bring tears to her eyes. He must have noticed her reaction, because he pulled her closer, releasing her hand so he could envelop her in his warmth and strength. She didn't resist, didn't even want to.

She had no reason on earth to deny herself this pleasure, nothing more to lose, so she met his kiss.

She savored the warmth of his mouth, loved his hands on her waist. Eliza was starving for affection, for attention… for someone to recognize and want her for who she was. This was her moment. Her tiny dash at satisfaction, and she meant to grab it.

* * *

Her Montana Man
Harlequin® Historical #923—December 2008

Praise for Cheryl St.John

"Ms. St.John knows what the readers want
and keeps on giving it."
—*Rendezvous*

"Ms. St.John holds a spot in my top-five list of
must-read Harlequin Historical authors. She is an
amazingly gifted author."
—*Writers Unlimited*

His Secondhand Wife
Nominated for a RITA® Award.
"A beautifully crafted and involving story about
the transforming power of love, this is
recommended reading."
—*Romantic Times BOOKreviews*

Prairie Wife
Nominated for a *Romantic Times BOOKreviews*
Reviewers' Choice Award.
"*Prairie Wife* is a very special book, courageously
executed by the author and her publisher.
Her considerable skill brings the common theme
of the romance novel—love conquers all—
to the level of genuine catharsis."
—*Romantic Times BOOKreviews* [4½ stars]

The Tenderfoot Bride
"Cheryl St.John once again touches the hearts of
readers… Not many readers will be able to hold back
their tears as they reach the conclusion."
—*Romance Reviews Today*

HER MONTANA MAN

CHERYL St. JOHN

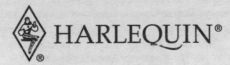

HARLEQUIN®

TORONTO • NEW YORK • LONDON
AMSTERDAM • PARIS • SYDNEY • HAMBURG
STOCKHOLM • ATHENS • TOKYO • MILAN • MADRID
PRAGUE • WARSAW • BUDAPEST • AUCKLAND

Recycling programs
for this product may
not exist in your area.

ISBN-13: 978-0-373-29523-4
ISBN-10:   0-373-29523-5

HER MONTANA MAN

www.eHarlequin.com

Printed in U.S.A.

With thanks and appreciation to the ladies who can't
eat as much chocolate as I can, but who definitely
help me out of the jams I write myself into and know
how to celebrate a birthday in style. Smooches to
Bernadette Duquette, Barb Hunt, Donna Knoell,
Debra Hines, Lizzie Starr, Chris Carter,
Sherri Shackelford and Julie Breese.

And thanks to Heartland Writers Group
for honoring my RWA milestone!

DON'T MISS THESE OTHER
NOVELS AVAILABLE NOW:

Chapter One

Silver Bend, Montana, May 1885

Jonas Black looked up from his ledgers and flipped open his ornately engraved gold pocket watch. Nearly three already. In preparation to leave his desk, he blotted the numbers he'd just tallied, then rubbed his ink-stained fingers on his denim trousers. There was something he did every afternoon at this time.

"Gonna be trouble at the North Star!" The tall stoop-shouldered man who tended bar rapped on Jonas's open office door at the same time as he shouted.

The North Star was the three-story hotel a few doors down, where Jonas and most of his employees lived. Jonas owned the hotel as well as the Silver Star Saloon.

"Tall fella, but not beefy," Quay told him. "He's hollerin' for Mrs. Holmes."

Jonas didn't bother to grab his jacket. He might talk this man into leaving peaceably, but experience had taught him it might take more than a simple *please* to appeal to an abuser. No call to ruin a perfectly good coat.

He glanced at the holstered Colt hanging on a peg just inside the door, but deliberately walked past and locked the door behind him.

With the shutters open to the warm afternoon sun, the saloon was warm and bright. The freshly scrubbed floors, the two patrons and the woman polishing the top of the mahogany bar barely registered as he strode for the door and out onto the shaded boardwalk.

"Madeline, come out here now! Don't make me come in and get you."

The stranger stood in the street, a sweaty bay tethered to the post in front of the hotel. His tailored black suit was coated with a layer of dust as though he'd been pushing the mare for the better part of a day. In Jonas's book, men who abused horses ranked right up there with men who mistreated women. Jonas had heard Madeline Holmes's story and drew the easy conclusion that this was the man she'd run from before finding refuge in Silver Bend.

"Don't make me come in there and drag you out!" the man shouted.

"Looking for someone?" Jonas called easily.

"Stay outta this, mister. Ain't none of your concern."

Jonas walked several yards toward the hotel. "Well, seems it is my concern since you're standing there hollerin' at the front windows of my establishment. State your business, Mister…"

"Baslow. This your hotel?"

"That it is. Jonas Black's the name. And you are?"

"I'm lookin' to take a woman back with me. I want Madeline Holmes."

"Is she your wife?"

The angry man deepened the scowl on his already craggy face, and his complexion reddened. "Ain't none of your damned business what she is. All you need to know is that she's comin' with me."

"I guess we can leave that up to Maddie, now, can't we?"

At Jonas's familiar use of her name, Baslow turned his whole body toward Jonas and squinted. "What's she to you?"

"A good employee. I'll go tell her you're here and you can ask her directly what she'd like to do."

The man jerked his head toward the saloon Jonas had exited. Quay still stood just outside the doors.

"She's in there?" Baslow shouted. "Whoring?"

Jonas gestured to a brightly painted wooden sign that hung on the outside of the building. "No sportin' women in my establishment. Maddie's one of my housekeepers."

"The hell you say. Madeline!" he roared, stalking toward the saloon.

Jonas frowned at Baslow's belligerent tone and aggressive stance. Eagerness for the man to try to push past him so he'd have reason to restrain him made his fingers tingle and his blood pump.

Instead, Baslow gave him a wide berth, striding to face the open saloon doors.

Casually, Jonas turned and stepped past Quay into the dim interior. This time his gaze sought and found the dark-haired woman who'd stopped polishing the bar and stood in rigid fear, her eyes as wide as saucers, her face pale. "Frank," she said on a dry rasp.

Jonas thought she might have been pretty once, before abuse and fear had added the appearance of more years to her narrow face. Using intimidation, the man had held her in his home and his bed for eight years. Breaking away had taken courage. Following through with her decision to escape would take even more.

"You don't have to be afraid," Jonas assured her. "Quay and I are right here. The whole of Silver Bend would see if he tried to force you away in plain sight. You don't have to go back with him. He can't make you. Tell him you don't want to leave. Make it loud 'n clear so there are witnesses."

Her frightened gaze moved from Jonas to the doorway. He'd seen the same bleak dread on too many faces, and it made his blood boil. "You're free, Maddie. You have a job and can take care of yourself. You don't need him. He has no control over you except what you give him. From here on out you can live your life any way you see fit. It's up to you."

His words took effect, and her expression changed. Madeline Holmes placed the cloth she'd been holding on the bar and, with precise movements, removed her apron, folded it neatly and set it down. She ran her palms over her skirt in a nervous gesture, then straightened and raised her chin. "He can't make me do anything I don't want to, can he?"

"No, he can't."

She walked toward the doors. Jonas followed.

As she stepped out onto the boardwalk, Baslow's severe gaze narrowed on her. His attention sidled over Jonas and Quay before fixing back on her as though the men were irritating flies he intended to swat later. "If you want to bring anything with you, get it now."

Her hands trembled, but with obvious deliberation she hid them in the folds of her skirts. Jonas cheered silently for her brave front.

"I have a job now. And my own room at the hotel," she said, her voice louder than he'd expected, though a slight tremble betrayed her nervousness. "I'm content to stay right here."

Baslow's thunderous expression darkened even more noticeably.

A few citizens had gathered on the boardwalk across the street and were watching the goings-on with interest. Wouldn't be the first time a fight had erupted in front of his place, Jonas thought, his blood pounding with keen awareness, and it wouldn't be the last. He had never minded a good fight to clear the air.

"You choosing a life of whoring over comin' with me?" Baslow bit out between clenched teeth.

Jonas kept his mouth shut. He'd already told the man there weren't any sporting women at his place, and everyone in town knew it. This was Maddie's chance to speak her piece.

"That's what I felt like when I was with you," she said, coming straight to the heart of the matter. "I don't want to live that way anymore. I'm not your wife." Her voice and demeanor showed renewed strength in her decision. "Nobody hits me," she declared. "And I get a fair wage for a day's work. I can take care of myself just fine."

Baslow headed toward Maddie. "I don't know who fed you that hogwash," he said, "but you belong to me, and you'll do as I say."

She backed away.

Jonas met him before he could reach the shade of the boardwalk. "Remember the brother's war, Baslow? It's against the law to keep slaves."

They stood three feet apart. Baslow's right eye twitched with anger. Jonas's palms tingled.

"Get outta my way, mister, before you regret it."

"Can't do that. Maddie's my employee, and I take care of my people."

Baslow lunged toward Jonas. Jonas dodged his first attempt to reach him, spinning with hands locked together to land a blow on the back of the man's neck.

Caught off guard, Baslow fell to his hands and knees in the dirt, losing his hat. Slowly, he shook his head, and then scrambled to his feet to come after Jonas. The fight was on.

The growing crowd pushed forward for a better look.

Energized now, Jonas raised both fists and bent his knees in readiness. Baslow faced him and they squared off, circling in avid concentration. The man's eyes bored into Jonas's with contempt. Jonas studied his stance, his movements, waited to see how he hit. Faster than Jonas anticipated, Baslow landed a blow to Jonas's shoulder that forced him to catch his balance and got him mad. He retaliated with a quick right that landed on the man's jaw with a crack and drew a grunt from his opponent and a murmur from the crowd.

Jonas didn't feel the hits that came next, though he knew one landed against his ribs and another at his temple. Adrenaline lent him strength and numbed the pain. In the minutes that followed he used the reprieve to his advantage, skillfully finding opportunities to put down punches.

Half-a-dozen solid hits later Baslow's lip was bleeding. He had a cut over his left eye, and he was breathing hard. Jonas watched for and found an opportunity, hit his eye again, then positioned all his muscle into landing a blow to his gut.

The man moaned and doubled over, dropping to his knees in the dirt. He glared up at Jonas, one eye red from streaming blood. "You got no right to keep Madeline."

"You're finally right," Jonas answered. "Nobody's got a right to hold her. She's free to leave, she's free to stay." He turned to Maddie, who'd been watching with both hands clasped under her chin. "You want to go?"

She shook her head and released a pent-up breath. "No."

"You sure? 'Cause we don't want any misunderstandin's. You're free to leave any time you want."

"I want to stay."

"There you have it." Jonas's knuckles were stinging now. "Need any more convincing?"

Marshal Haglar parted the crowd and made his way to stand on the brick street a few feet away. He took in both men's appearances. "What in blazes is goin' on here?"

Maddie immediately ran forward to explain what had taken place. When she'd finished, the marshal turned to the spectators. "That how it happened? Anyone see the whole thing?"

Jonas couldn't remember if anyone had been there during the initial exchange of words. He scanned the faces nearby. People had an aversion to getting involved, especially when a dangerous-looking fellow like Baslow glared at them as though daring someone to speak against him.

The marshal eyed the crowd, and one after another, the bystanders glanced at the person beside them and then away. Jonas figured his reputation and position on the town council would have enough sway. He wasn't a troublemaker, but he never ran from a fight, either. He didn't want to put Warren Haglar in a bad position, and the indifference of the locals irritated him.

Townspeople turned as movement caught their attention, and Jonas looked, too. From the opposite boardwalk, a slender woman in a blue-and-white gingham dress and a straw hat held the hem of her skirts above her shoes and stepped down onto the paving bricks. She walked to within four feet of the law officer. An unexpected tremor stabbed at Jonas's belly.

"I saw the entire incident, Marshal," she said. "I saw that man ride up and shout for Mrs. Holmes."

Of course. *Jonas's three o'clock obsession.* She'd been on the boardwalk the whole time. Eliza Jane Sutherland was rather tall for a woman, and on the rare occasion that she'd been without a hat, he'd seen that her hair was black and glossy in the sunlight. Jonas had never heard her speak more than a one- or two-word greeting, so now her magnificent silky voice, more than the words she spoke, caught and held his attention.

"Mr. Black came out of his establishment and suggested that he—" she pointed to the scowling stranger "—leave." Her bright amber gaze moved to Jonas.

Something in his chest throbbed at the direct look, something ragged and weighty, something more alarming than facing a dozen angry men in the street.

The marshal asked her several questions and she replied directly. Jonas couldn't take his eyes from her.

Every afternoon, rain or shine, Eliza Jane walked to the small tea shop that was a red brick storefront nestled on the corner beside Earl Mobley's tailor shop on the opposite side of the street. Once inside, she seated herself at a table before the front window, where Bonnie Jacobson brought her a china cup and a pot of tea. Most days Jonas observed her ritual from just inside the door of the saloon where she couldn't see him, but occasionally he found a reason to run an errand to the hardware store across the street in time for her arrival.

Once or twice he'd paused on the boardwalk as she passed and tipped his hat. As soon as she'd raised those amber eyes, his heart thudded in his chest and he'd chastised himself. Nothing and no one intimidated Jonas Black.

Apparently the marshal had no problem accepting the true story now that Eliza Jane had verified it, because he turned to Baslow. "Time you moved on."

Baslow shot Maddie a look of seething rage. "You ain't seen the last of me, woman. Don't think your friends can protect you forever."

"Anything happens to Miss Holmes, and we'll know who to look for," the marshal told him. "I'll be wiring the county seat to let 'em know about this disturbance."

Baslow located his hat where it lay in the street. He snatched it up, whacked it against his thigh and settled it on his head before walking toward his horse and untying it. From the clumsy way he mounted, Jonas suspected he was masking a couple of cracked ribs.

Marshal Haglar watched as the man turned his mount away and galloped out of town. "Stay out of sight, but follow him a ways to make sure he's headed home," he told one of the young men who had a horse tethered across the street.

Once Baslow was out of sight and the man he'd sent was tailing him, the marshal approached Maddie.

"Thank you, Marshal," she said.

"I had the easy part," he replied. "Looks like Jonas got the worst of it."

Maddie looked Jonas over, but after noting the onlookers, a tinge of embarrassment stained her cheeks. "Sorry," she said low enough that only Jonas and the marshal could hear.

"You handled it perfectly," Jonas told her. "You had a crowd of witnesses while Frank was bullyin' you, and when you stood up for yourself, you gained the respect of each one. He can't hurt you anymore."

He could tell the moment when it no longer mattered that she'd been humiliated on a public street. Maddie had just gained respect for herself. She caught her bottom lip with her teeth, but couldn't hold back a smile. She brought her palms to her blazing cheeks. "I shouldn't be so pleased when you're standing there bleeding."

He looked down at his knuckles, which had taken to throbbing like the very dickens.

The marshal tipped his hat. "Afternoon, Miss Holmes," he said as though they'd just encountered each other on the boardwalk.

"Marshal."

Jonas searched the crowd and noted that Eliza Jane had returned to the other side of the street. She was just entering the tea shop. Well, hell. He'd had the perfect reason to speak to her and had let it slip by. Now he was going to have to go after her. His stomach lurched. Confused the tar out of him why that thought was scarier than anything that had happened so far.

"Come in and put some ice on your hands," Maddie suggested.

"I'll be right there." He gestured for her to go back to the Silver Star without him and crossed the street. He needed to thank the witness for verifying his story.

Chapter Two

A couple of the men spoke to him, commenting on the incident. The last few remaining townsfolk headed back to their jobs and errands.

Jonas moved on, pausing outside the tearoom, his ink-stained and bleeding fingers on the door handle. Scoffing at his uncharacteristic hesitation, he walked in, surprised to hear the delicate tinkle of a bell. It rang again as he closed the door and glanced around. Silence and the scents of cinnamon and spices engulfed him. He couldn't imagine feeling more out of place.

Eliza Jane had taken a seat at her usual table by the window and removed her straw hat. Bonnie had just set a fancy rose-patterned cup and saucer on the pristine white tablecloth. Eliza Jane watched him cross the room toward her. His boot heels were glaringly loud on the wood floor. Her amber eyes held surprise…and wariness.

"I wanted to thank you…for speaking up the way

you did," he said. She held his gaze, and he got that funny feeling in his belly.

"I simply told the marshal what I'd seen."

"A lot of people wouldn't have done that with Baslow standing right there glarin' at them."

She shrugged. "I did it for the woman."

Jonas nodded. "You did a good thing."

Bonnie bustled from the back room with a cloth in her outstretched hand. He knew her from the town council meetings, since she ran her own business and most often attended. "Put this on your cheek there, Jonas. And come to the back and wash those hands."

He accepted the wet cloth and touched it to his cheek where numbness had been replaced by a stinging sensation. Some impression he must be making, standing there bleeding. Coming here probably hadn't been his wisest choice. "I'm not gonna bleed on your tablecloths, Bonnie. I'm not stayin'. I just wanted to thank Miss Sutherland."

"I wasn't worried about the tablecloths, I was concerned about your face and hands."

"I'm all right."

"You want a cup of tea?"

"No, thanks."

She glanced at Eliza and back at him. "All right then. I'll bring your tea right out, Eliza Jane."

Once they were alone again, she met Jonas's gaze. "Is that woman, the one he was after, is she your...I mean are you two...?"

Her blunt question surprised him. He shook his head. "Maddie works for me. She warned me about Baslow, so I knew what to expect. Nobody has a right to push another person around just because they're bigger or stronger. The man had worse comin' to him."

Eliza studied the man standing in front of her with a new perspective. She'd seen him on the street a few times, knew of him and his enterprises, but they'd never had occasion to speak. Her brother-in-law had no use for Jonas Black, calling him a slave trader because he sold employment forms to itinerant workers seeking jobs. Silver Bend was a thoroughfare between the States and the British border, and scores of men sought work with threshing crews, in logging camps and orchards, even mines.

She knew about hiring migrant workers. She'd worked in her father's brickyard since she'd been old enough to dig clay. Later she'd handled bookkeeping and accounts with enough skill to help buy railroad and bank shares. She'd managed the finances until well after her father's death—until her sister's health declined and Jenny Lee needed her more and more. Now she spent her days caring for her invalid sister and her young nephew.

No doubt about it, there were unscrupulous employment agencies. Many times workers had shown up at The Sutherland Brick Company to find out that two or three times as many forms as there were positions had been sold. Eliza didn't know if this man was one of those agents or not. His father had been the town doctor for a good many years. Rumor had it that Dr. Black's wife had been killed and he'd never gotten over it.

Bonnie brought Eliza Jane's pot of tea. "Piping hot,"

she said, placing it on the table. "Care for a cup?" she asked Jonas.

"Thanks, no," he said with a shake of his head.

Bonnie headed back to the kitchen.

Jonas had left Silver Bend years ago, and since his return Eliza hadn't had opportunity to do more than see him in passing. She didn't have much firsthand knowledge at all, except that he was polite whenever he greeted her. It was common knowledge that he owned and ran the saloon and the hotel, and she'd never heard anyone other than her brother-in-law speak poorly of him.

She had learned one thing today, however. Without hesitation for his own safety, he had protected the Holmes woman from a man she obviously feared. The way he'd stood up to her tormenter spoke volumes about Jonas's character.

"You should probably take care of that hand," she said.

He glanced down at his knuckles. A nasty gash and blue-tinged swelling were evidence of the pain Baslow would be feeling for a while to come. Jonas flexed his fingers with a nod. "It'll be fine."

Bonnie returned with a rose-patterned plate holding a frosted tea cake.

Jonas glanced from Eliza to Bonnie. "Ladies."

Eliza nodded a farewell.

"Jonas," Bonnie replied.

He turned and exited the shop. The bell tinkled twice, echoing into the subsequent silence.

"What do you make of that?" Bonnie asked.

Eliza looked at her, puzzled.

"I've seen the man toe-to-toe with miscreants before, but I've never known him to set foot in here. You must've made a powerful impression."

"I don't know about that," she replied, quickly looking down and stirring sugar into her tea.

"How is Jenny Lee today?" Bonnie asked, changing the subject.

"Sit down for a few minutes," Eliza invited, then tasted the lemon-frosted pastry and dabbed her lips with her napkin. "It's a fair day, as her days go."

Bonnie sat with her hands folded under her chin, studying Eliza. "And she still insists that you take time for yourself every afternoon."

Eliza picked up her cup and blew across the surface of the fragrant liquid. "She's concerned she's a burden. Of course she's not, but she says the least I deserve is an hour a day to myself. I come to walk Tyler home from school anyway, so I may as well arrive in town a little early." She glanced at the brooch timepiece pinned to her dress. "My time's been cut short today."

She took her coin purse from her pocket.

"Your refreshments are complimentary today." Bonnie extended a hand to prevent Eliza from producing a coin. "You barely had time to enjoy it."

"Regardless, you brewed it."

"You're my best customer," Bonnie argued. "I can give you a cup of tea now and then if I like."

Eliza smiled and picked up her hat. "Thank you."

After Bonnie walked her to the door, she exited the

shop and headed east. Nearly every structure along Main Street was made of brick. Prior to firing them, she could remember stamping the bricks, like those that comprised Brauman's Leather Goods, alongside her father and three other men.

A loaded wagon rumbled past. Eight years ago they'd sold the bricks that paved the street for a dollar seventeen a thousand. She'd overseen each wagon that left the yard. She'd be leaving a part of her behind when she left this town.

Eliza abandoned Main Street for the open lots between the businesses and the school yard. Three weeks of sun and little rain had dried ground that had been soggy from melted snow only a month ago. Reaching the shade of an ancient sycamore, she sat on the grass, tucking her skirts around her, to await dismissal.

Four years ago she'd persuaded the town council to replace the wood frame schoolhouse with brick by telling them of the hazard from flying sparks cast by the woodstove. They'd insisted on painting the building white, and she'd had no problem with that as long as the children were safe. She'd supervised construction herself, as well as donated half the bricks, plus a fireplace and chimney.

A team and wagon driven by a young farmhand in a straw hat rolled to a stop near the sound little structure. The same fellow came to town each day to collect sons and daughters from outlying farms. School remained in session until fall when the children were needed to work in the fields.

The door opened. Miss Fletcher used a hook and eye from the door to the rail on the banister to hold it open. A line of children streamed from the building into the sunlight, some running, others chatting with friends.

Tyler's pale blond hair stood out from the others', and Eliza Jane's heart swelled with tenderness as it had every time she'd seen him since the moment he was born.

He walked between two other boys, their heads bent over something Timmy Hatcher held in his cupped palm. Timmy spoke and Tyler and the other boy nodded and laughed.

Eliza stood and walked to the hard dirt path that led from the school toward town. Girls with braids passed with shy greetings.

Tyler looked up and spotted her waiting. He said a hasty goodbye to his friends and continued forward. He used to run to her, eager for a hug, but he would turn eight his next birthday, and he saved his hugs for bedtime now. She extended a hand, but he pretended he didn't see it and walked beside her, two books under his arm.

"Did Miss Fletcher give two assignments for this evening?" she asked.

"Yep. The arithmetic is hard, too."

"Fortunate for you, you're such a smart boy," she replied.

He nodded in all seriousness. "Mikey Kopeke has a harder time. And his dad don't let him do his homework cause he has chores."

"A lot of the children have chores," she said. "Their

parents need them to help with the animals and the crops more than they need them to memorize times tables."

"Papa says when you know your times tables and letters you don't have to work so hard all your life."

Eliza Jane felt a little sick, the way she always did at the sight or mention of Royce Dunlap. "Papa's right about getting a good education," she told him. Tyler loved Eliza Jane's brother-in-law with the fierce loyalty a boy felt for his father, even though Royce was forever preoccupied with new business ventures and office matters. More often than not her heart ached for Tyler. No child should go through what he had with an ill mother and an emotionally distant father. Especially not this child.

"Mama's having a pretty good day today," she told him, trying to sound assuring. Days like this were so much easier on him.

"But she won't get better," he said, without looking at her.

Her chest ached at the truth as well as the fact that someone so young and vulnerable had to face it. It was unfair that he had to learn about life this way. "No, Tyler. She won't get better."

He glanced up at her then, his blue eyes sad and trusting. If she could change the world for this boy, she would. She hated feeling helpless. She hated feeling responsible.

But most of all, Eliza hated feeling guilty.

Chapter Three

It was a warm sunlit afternoon, and they walked the rest of the way home in silence, pausing at the wrought iron gate to admire Sutherland's finest cherry-red brick, the clean lines of the white window caps and functional green shutters. Eliza loved the irregular Italianate architecture. There were two stories and an attic in the main section and two stories in the jutting side section where the sitting and dining rooms were down and an immense sunroom up. In front, the main part featured a jutting two-story section with windows on three sides on each floor and a balcony atop.

A Queen Anne porch had been added for her mother several years after the original construction. The home and its rooms held memories of her parents and many good times when her sister was young and not feeble. They were memories Eliza treasured, even though her heart broke with each recall. They entered the house, and she sent Tyler upstairs for time alone with Jenny Lee.

Nora Cahill, their neighbor, greeted Tyler on her way down the stairs to the foyer. She turned to watch him climb to the top and disappear along the hallway to Jenny Lee's room. Nora turned a saddened gaze on Eliza. "I don't even know what to say to the child anymore."

Eliza's parents had lived in this house from the time Eliza had been a toddler, and Nora and her husband had lived next door all those years. As children she and Jenny Lee had played with Nora's daughter, Vernelle, who had eventually married and moved East. When Eliza's mother's heart had weakened and she had lingered for weeks, Nora had been a blessing. Years later Nora had comforted the adult sisters when their father had died.

"None of us thought Jenny Lee would hold on this long. Your mother used to dread her dying. Maybe it's best she's not here for the end."

Eliza loved Nora like an aunt, but that comment silenced her. She would much rather have her mother alive today, no matter what.

"Thank you for these afternoons," she said with heartfelt gratitude. If Jenny Lee hadn't insisted a year ago that Eliza take an hour to herself each day, there would probably be weeks at a stretch that she never left the house or her sister's side. She needed the nourishing time to draw on inner strength, to think and to plan.

And she had a plan.

"You know I'm happy to come over any time," Nora told her. "I left a couple loaves of bread rising. You can bake them later."

Eliza leaned to give her a quick hug and then saw her to the door. Closing it, she turned to gaze up the stairway. It had grown more and more difficult to keep a cheerful attitude and guard her expression. Her sister looked nothing like the fun-loving, lovely young girl Eliza wanted to remember, but she steadfastly held her sorrow at bay. Jenny and Tyler needed her now more than ever.

After a difficult moment, she drew a fortifying breath, gathered her skirts and purposefully trod one stair at a time. The worn banister was familiar and comforting to her touch. She knew the number of steps and which ones creaked. The house was her solace, her haven. She could find her way around in the pitch dark without effort. The thought of leaving had always been too much to bear…until now. Any comfort she'd once drawn here had been spoiled by her brother-in-law's presence.

The door to Jenny Lee's room was always open unless Royce went in to visit her alone, which happened rarely anymore. A year ago, he'd moved to another room down the hall. Eliza had offered to bring a cot for him if he was afraid of disturbing his wife's rest; she had even suggested two smaller beds instead of the one that had been her parents', but he declined.

She thought he could have been more attentive and helpful. His moving from the room caused Eliza more work. Now she needed to check on her sister throughout the night. But she'd learned that defying Royce's decisions and demands only caused more trouble, and she had to keep things calm for Jenny Lee's sake.

Tyler was sitting on the side of the bed, his expression animated as he finished telling Jenny Lee something about Timmy Hatcher. Jenny's adoring smile was already thin. As much as she loved to hear about Tyler's day and cling to those last vestiges of normal life, she could only mask the pain and fatigue for brief spells. When she saw Eliza Jane, regret and relief warred in her sunken eyes.

Immediately interpreting unspoken clues, Tyler kissed Jenny Lee's cheek before easing himself to stand beside the bed. "I'll come back to see you after supper, Mama."

"I love you, Tyler. You don't know how much."

"I love you, too, Mama."

The sisters watched him leave the room, and then their eyes met. Jenny Lee's held tears.

"Do you need your medicine?" Eliza asked.

"Please."

She fed Jenny two teaspoons of the elixir Dr. McKee provided for pain, then helped her turn on her side and adjusted a few pillows for comfort. Eliza pulled the chair close beside the bed and took a seat.

Jenny Lee reached for her hand. Her sister's cool fingers felt alarmingly slim and frail and Eliza was always afraid of hurting her. Jenny was wearing a smile, though, when Eliza's gaze rose to her face. Her skin was unnaturally translucent and white, her eyes too shiny.

"Remember when we were girls, Liza, and we couldn't wait to get home from school with Vernelle? We'd all go up into the attic room and play for hours. Mother used to shoo us out of doors for fresh air, and we'd take the same fantasy game we'd been playing to Nora's backyard behind those big lilac bushes."

"I remember," Eliza answered. Nora had brought bouquets of lilacs from those very bushes into Jenny Lee's room all that spring. "You always wore Grandma Pritchard's rose evening dress and the bead necklace."

"Those were *pearls,*" Jenny Lee insisted. "And *you* liked Mother's blue dress with the ruffled sleeves."

"We were quite the fashionable ladies, weren't we?"

"I felt rather deserted when Vernelle married Robert and moved East," Jenny Lee confided.

"As did Nora."

"And then I married Royce." Jenny Lee's gaze wandered away for a few moments and then returned. "Did you feel I'd deserted you?"

"Of course not. You were only across the neighborhood."

Royce and Jenny Lee had rented a small home. Shortly after Henry Sutherland's death, Jenny Lee's health had declined to where she needed more and more attention, and she was unable to care for Tyler. Moving here had been the practical and necessary thing for all of them. Eliza had quit her bookkeeping position at the brickyard and devoted herself to her sister and Tyler. She'd never been sorry, and she never would be.

Confirmation of Royce's true nature had come soon after. The truth of what she'd suspected for some time had been unraveled in startling increments and ugly realizations. Eliza covered up his disinterest in Jenny Lee and Tyler to protect them. Her sister was dying.

She didn't need the hurt of knowing her husband had married her to get his hands on The Sutherland Brick Company and their other investments.

Henry had left a portion of the business to each of them, and they'd had equal say in decisions. Most often Royce had been able to sway Jenny Lee to his point of view on investments and holdings, and Eliza hadn't been willing to fight him in front of her sister. The few times she'd tried, the hurt look on Jenny Lee's face had discouraged her.

She didn't want to plan for her sister's death, but she had to be realistic. Once Jenny Lee was out of the triangle, Royce would own the major share of the brick-yard and could do whatever he pleased.

His intentions didn't stop there. A shudder ran up her spine and infused her with ominous panic. With controlled effort, she fought down the feeling.

Eliza Jane had a plan.

She'd stashed away and hidden her savings—not in the bank, because they owned a share of the bank and Royce could look at accounts anytime he wanted. But in a safer place. When the inevitable time came to escape, she would be able to take care of herself and Tyler.

"Remember how Father used to read to us in the evenings?" Jenny Lee asked, and Eliza was grateful to return to a happier time with her. "Mama would sit in that brown wing chair and work on her quilts while he read us stories. He was a good father, wasn't he?"

Eliza sensed the disappointment her sister felt that her husband had never been a caring or loving father to

Tyler. It had always seemed to Eliza that he'd tolerated the boy just to pacify Jenny Lee and her father. Now she knew it was so.

"It's so unfair that I got this puny heart," Jenny said with a catch in her voice. She rarely spoke in such a hopeless fashion.

"I'm going to take care of Tyler." Eliza looked right into her sister's eyes and assured her.

Jenny Lee squeezed her hand without much strength. "I know you will." The medicine had taken its effect, and her eyes drifted closed. "I'm going to rest for a few minutes."

Her lashes lay against the dark hollows under her eyes. With her blue eyes closed, she didn't even look like herself. Eliza often washed and curled her hair, but it was thin and lank. Eliza swallowed a painful lump in her throat and fought tears. A show of emotion wouldn't help a thing. Strength would.

"I love you, Liza." Jenny hadn't opened her eyes, for which Eliza was grateful. Pain was sure to be evident on her face.

"I love you, Jenny."

Once she was sure her sister slept comfortably, she slipped out of the room. In the hall, she stood with her back against the wall, a great weight crushing her heart, and the pull of tears threatening her last shreds of composure. As sorrow washed over her in cresting waves, she clasped both hands to her breast, and pressed her fingers to her lips to hold back sobs. If she started now, she would never stop.

After several minutes, she took a deep breath, collected herself and made her way downstairs. She found Tyler working on his arithmetic assignments in the kitchen. She stoked the oven and checked the temperature to bake the bread. "I remember sitting here doing my schoolwork when I was your age."

Jenny's talk had kindled memories, and Eliza ached for happy carefree times. Jenny Lee had never been strong, not even then, but the seriousness of her heart condition hadn't been apparent. They'd simply been two young girls with two parents, sharing the comfortable home their father had built for them and that their mother ran with aplomb.

"And Mama, too? Did she do her arithmetic right here?"

"That she did." She cut him a wedge of cheese and poured him a cup of milk.

"Is she as good at numbers as you are, Aunt Eliza?"

Eliza put on a kettle of water for tea and sat across from him. "Her strengths tend to lie in word studies, subjects like spelling and English. As I recall she was very good at geography, as well. We always dreamed about the faraway places we would see one day."

"Did you ever?"

She studied his fingers on the pencil. "No. We never traveled farther than Denver."

"Maybe we could all go."

They sat in silence for a few minutes. He had confirmed his understanding that Jenny Lee would not get better, but did he truly comprehend that she was going to die?

A stab of pity snatched her breath and formed an aching knot in her chest. He was too young to learn this particular life lesson. "Tyler," she said, approaching the subject cautiously. "You understand that Mama is very, very sick, don't you?"

He nodded, keeping his gaze on his paper.

"And you know that…" She pursed her lips to keep them from trembling. "You know she won't be with us much longer."

He didn't look up. "She's gonna die."

"Yes." She barely managed a whisper.

"She told me."

Eliza studied the curve of his cheek, the delicate sweep of his pale eyelashes and experienced a swell of love. Of course her sister had prepared him. Jenny Lee loved him more than life. Again, she blinked back the sting of tears.

At last he raised those bright blue eyes to hers. Eyes as earnest and clear as Jenny Lee's had once been. "She said not to be afraid 'cause you'd take care of me always. Will you?"

Nothing could stop her. Nothing. And no one. She got up and placed her cheek against his. "Of course I will. Always. I promise."

Jenny Lee didn't have much appetite, but that evening Eliza managed to get her to sip a cup of broth and take some tea before giving her the medicine and making her comfortable.

She had tucked Tyler into bed and returned downstairs where she sorted laundry in the washroom beyond the kitchen. She sent out bedding and most of the clothing, but she washed her own and Jenny's Lee's delicate garments herself. She packed the laundry into bags, which would be picked up the following morning, and set her wash load aside.

A sound alerted her to her brother-in-law's presence, and her senses went on alert. Alarm prickled along the skin on her arms and neck. She stepped to the doorway.

Royce stood on the far side of the kitchen. His shrewd gaze crawled over her. He was dressed as impeccably as always in a dark coat and white shirt, his brown hair parted so that it waved away from his forehead. "I'll take my supper now."

"I'll get your plate from the oven." She walked around the opposite side of the table and grabbed one of the flour sacks Nora had layered and sewn for protection from hot pot handles.

Royce's boot heels struck the wood floor in a rapid cadence a split second before he reached her.

She whirled to face him, her body stiff.

He stopped inches from her. He wore closely trimmed sideburns and a ribbon-thin mustache on the very edge of his upper lip.

Eliza turned her face to the side to avoid his unbearable nearness and drilling gaze. His breath touched her chin. Hairs rose on her neck and arm.

"You're looking lovely tonight."

"You're married to my sister."

"A tenuous bond at the very least."

Her heart thundered against her rib cage. "How can you treat her death so callously?"

He leaned forward without actually touching her until his heat scorched her cheek and seared her body. "It's business, my dear."

The sensation of being trapped sent a shudder of revulsion along her spine. She closed her eyes in the futile hope that she'd open them to find this encounter had only been another menacing nightmare.

"Don't be so priggish, Eliza Jane. You're no unblemished paragon of virtue." She started at the touch of his finger as he ran it along her jaw. "I expect you'll be quite an enthusiastic partner once you've resigned yourself to the next phase of our relationship."

"We don't have a relationship."

"Ah, but we will." His hand circled her wrist, and she spun away from him then, escaping from the heat of the oven behind her and his menacing overtures.

She darted to the opposite side of the table and stood with her hands on the spindles of the chair back, bile rising in her throat. "You disgust me."

"I find the chase quite titillating, actually." With a swagger, he moved to a chair and seated himself before the place setting she'd prepared. He adjusted the cutlery in precise alignment before leveling a warning gaze on her. "Don't get carried away, however. There's a time and a place for everything, and soon your time for coy resistance will run out. Once Jenny Lee is gone and we've served a respectable mourning period, you will become my wife."

Eliza stood with her heart in her throat, trapped in

this house and under this man's rule for the time being. She couldn't leave Jenny Lee or Tyler. They needed her. He knew it. And he used her love for them to his advantage.

"It's the natural course of things in anyone's eyes," he added.

A hundred nights she'd lain awake into the wee hours of morning, listening for him, dreading his next move, imagining endless scenarios of telling Jenny Lee the ugly truth, of going to the marshal, yet always coming to the same hopeless conclusion: she could not break Jenny Lee's heart. She would never let her sister know that Royce had married her for a percent of the brickyard...and that he was awaiting her death to amass the final ownership.

Once that happened, he would have control. All Eliza could do was bide her time and endure. Shelter her sister. Protect Tyler. And avoid this deplorable excuse for a human being until—until their situation changed.

She moved to the oven, took out the hot plate and set it in front of him while guardedly keeping her distance. Sometimes she was so angry with her father for allowing this to happen that she didn't know what to do with those feelings.

"You're quite transparent, Eliza Jane," he said. "But resenting me isn't going to do any good." He picked up his fork and knife and sliced the roast. "We both know why you'll comply." He took a bite and chewed before looking up at her again. "But you've already figured that out, haven't you?"

Her heart skipped a beat.

Anger distorted her vision for seconds and she clenched her teeth, unable to speak.

"You have no legal rights to Tyler unless you marry me."

"You aren't human," she finally replied, venom lacing her tone.

"And you will marry me. Because I have knowledge that will hurt both of you. And you don't want me to tell."

"I could kill you in your sleep," she said. And God help her, she'd already thought of it. But she was too much of a coward. What if she went to jail and left Tyler here alone?

Royce actually smiled, something he did rarely, and she suspected it was because one of his front teeth overlapped the other. "I shall remember to sleep lightly."

Why should he sleep any better than she?

Once Jenny Lee was gone, Eliza would be forced to put her plan into action, take Tyler and escape. This house her father had built, the town she called home, all the precious memories, none of it mattered as much as protecting Tyler.

The bell on the front door screeched as a visitor twisted the handle. Relieved at the interruption, Eliza tossed down the towel and hurried to answer the call.

A young man in a flannel jacket and mended dungarees stood on the porch holding a fistful of white daisies. "Miss Sutherland?"

"Yes."

"These is for you." He thrust the bouquet into her hands and turned away.

"Wait!" she called, but he was already out the gate and running down the street, where dusk was turning Silver Bend to shades of gold and deep lavender. She glanced at the rocky buttes in the distance, then down at the flowers she held.

"Who was it?"

Royce stood behind her. She turned to meet his thunderous expression. He spotted the bouquet. "Who sent those?"

"I don't know."

She spotted the small note tucked between the blooms at the same time he did. He snatched the card, catching several delicate white petals that fell to the polished wood at their feet.

Royce read the note, then his ominous gaze rose to level on her. He set his mouth in a disapproving line and grabbed the bunch of flowers from her hand. "Don't be getting any ideas. You'll be sorry if you cross me."

He threw the daisies to the floor and crushed them beneath the heel of his boot, grinding until stems and petals and leaves were a mass of ruin.

With deliberate intimidation, he tore the note into pieces and tossed it onto the debris.

"I want coffee in the study after I've eaten." He turned and walked back toward the kitchen.

Confused, Eliza looked down at the trampled flowers. She would have to get a broom and dustpan. Kneeling, she picked up the strewn scraps of paper and fitted them together on the floor like a jigsaw puzzle.

The handwriting was square and neat, unfamiliar.

"Hopefully these will make a better impression," she read. No signature. Nothing that should have angered Royce to the degree it had. But then he didn't need much prompting.

She tucked the bits of paper into the pocket of her skirt. No signature had been required for her to know the daisies had come from Jonas Black. He'd already thanked her for telling the marshal what she'd seen. This gesture had been unnecessary…but she found it touchingly kind.

There was no way Royce could have known who sent the bouquet. He'd have been even angrier if he'd suspected they'd come from the "slave trader," the man she'd seen fighting in the street that day.

Jonas had sent flowers. She didn't know what to make of that, but she didn't have the time or energy to figure it out. She had too much to handle right here. A faint regret for what she could never have, tried to edge its way into her thinking.

The rapid echo of bare feet in the upstairs hall drew her attention, and she lifted her gaze to see Tyler slide to a halt and grip the banister. "Aunt Eliza!" he called down, his young voice squeaking with urgency. "Come quick! It's Mama!"

Chapter Four

Just because Eliza had known the time was coming didn't make her sister's death any easier to accept. She hadn't had any close friends since grade school; Jenny had been her friend. They had shared everything—or nearly everything. There at the end, Eliza had kept Royce's true nature a secret. She suspected Jenny had been disappointed, but she'd been as brave about her disenchantment with her marriage as she had about her illness.

The past two days had been a blur. Now that the funeral service was over and she'd ridden home with Tyler and Royce, Eliza remembered that she hadn't eaten that day. She tried to recall if she'd eaten the day before and assumed she must have. Upon hanging up her shawl, she hurried past the rooms where furniture had been moved and chairs arranged, to the back of the house. A few of the ladies from church were already setting out food.

The aromas of savory beef, apples and cinnamon, and freshly brewed coffee would normally have teased her appetite, but today they made her feel queasy. She surveyed the abundance of food on the table. "Oh my goodness!"

"I think everyone in town brought something." Penny Wright stepped close. Eliza and Penny had handled many a meal such as this in their duties as members of the Ladies' Aid Society, but Eliza couldn't remember seeing this much food since her father's funeral. The Sutherlands were well thought of. She pressed a hand to her midriff as if the touch could hold back the pain of loss and the poignant appreciation for her neighbors' thoughtfulness.

Penny wrapped an arm around Eliza's shoulders, giving her a comforting squeeze. Realizing she'd never hug her sister again, Eliza's chest throbbed with a hollow ache. Pulling a lace-edged hankie from her pocket, she dabbed her nose and focused on the dining room table with all the leaves in place. The ivory lace cloth that had been her mother's was now nearly hidden by steaming casseroles and delectable-looking cakes and pies. This was the day she had dreaded and welcomed at the same time.

Footsteps sounded behind her, and Eliza turned as Nora entered the room, carrying yet another covered dish. Penny scurried to make a spot for it.

Nora took Eliza's hand and squeezed her fingers. Her pale face and puffy eyes showed evidence of the strain she shared. Eliza used the same strength Penny had offered to give her friend a hug. They'd already heard a plethora of trite things people said at a time like this. Jenny Lee's suffering was over. She was in a better place. But mere words couldn't fix the pain or emptiness left by this unfair loss, so they shared a silent moment of grief.

A rap sounded on the front door. Eliza straightened and tucked her hankie into her sleeve in preparation.

Two and three at a time, the men and women of Silver Bend arrived in their Sunday best and milled about waiting for the reverend to pray over the meal. Reverend Miller finally parted the crowd in the parlor and gave a brief blessing. Penny directed mourners to the sideboard, which was stacked with plates and flatware.

Nora cupped Eliza's elbow. "Let's get you a plate."

"Tyler—" Eliza began.

"Marian is taking care of Tyler."

She allowed Nora to walk her through the line and fill a plate for her. The woman ushered her to a chair in the parlor. "Now sit and take some nourishment."

Eliza accepted the plate without noting what it held. As always, Nora's presence was a blessing. It would be impossible to thank her for all she'd done for their family, but Eliza would have to find some small way to show her appreciation. A special and meaningful gesture was a must. She scanned the gathering and found Tyler sitting on the wide brick hearth with Timmy Hatcher and Michael Kopeke. Miss Fletcher sat nearby, wearing a smile and engaging them in conversation.

His life would go on. Eliza's life would go on. They had to learn to make that happen without Jenny Lee. And some way—without Royce.

From the other room his voice broke through her reverie. The mere sound made her skin crawl. He was talking about the Horace Vernet painting in the hallway, the one her father had purchased during a trip he and her mother had taken abroad many years ago. Royce spoke of the French painter and the history of the piece as though he had something to do with it. As though it was his.

Nora had always admired that painting. Eliza took a bite of Delores Cress's signature stroganoff, knowing it tasted better than sawdust, but she had no appetite.

"Miss Sutherland."

She drew her gaze upward from a pair of polished black boots to pressed black trousers, past a matching tailored coat and smart bow tie before recognizing Jonas Black. She set down her fork. "Mr. Black."

Eliza Jane attempted to rise, but Jonas stopped her with an outstretched hand and seated himself on the chair beside hers. Her usually luminous skin was pale and her eyes showed she hadn't slept. She probably hadn't eaten, and here he was interrupting her meal.

"I'll get a plate and join you." He hurried through the wide opening to the hall and found the dining room, returning a few minutes later. "You won't have to cook for a week."

"Everyone feels helpless," she answered. "They want to do something."

He nodded and took a bite of chocolate-frosted cake, even though there was plenty of other food on his plate. He caught her looking and grinned sheepishly. "Sweet tooth."

Side by side, they ate in silence. He finished, and Delores Cress came by to take his plate and return with a cup of coffee. "Thank you, ma'am."

Eliza held her half-empty plate out to Delores.

"Would you like coffee?" the other woman asked. "I have water on and can make you some tea."

"No, thank you."

Jonas sipped the brew, then turned to find a spot on a side table to set the cup. He leveled his gaze on Eliza. "When my father died, you were one of the ladies servin' food and coffee."

She didn't meet his eyes. "I remember."

He looked away, searching his mind for words. "I recall your kindness that day. You told me that my father was a good man and that you would miss him."

"He was a good man." Her gaze rose to his then. "And I've missed him. He was kind to my family. Diligent. He always came out day or night, rain or shine to take care of Jenny or my parents."

"That day...I knew you understood," he told her, "that words were inadequate. You didn't say all the things people normally say at a time like that. You had already lost your mother."

Eliza shrugged. "Words are cheap. It's what we do that determines who we are."

Her straightforward manner surprised him, but he

admired her practical philosophy. He wondered if she was thinking about him fighting Baslow in the street the other day, wondered if she thought that scuffle defined who he was.

Her gaze was steady, sending the same disturbing feeling it always elicited across his nerve endings. Why was it her presence made him look into himself with questions? *Did* that fight define him?

She unsettled him.

"Thank you for the flowers." Her cheeks turned pink, bringing fresh color to her pale complexion. She held his gaze only a moment longer, then glanced away, confirming her embarrassment.

"Appreciate that you spoke up," he answered.

"You'd already thanked me."

He had. But the words hadn't felt adequate. Well, truth was he'd groped for an opportunity to paint himself in a better light in her mind. Why in tarnation he gave it a second thought was a concern, though.

Across the room, a woman spoke to a youngster, and he rose from where he sat on the hearth to leave with her. The remaining platinum-haired boy stared after them, then his gaze moved across the people crowding the room toward the hallway. Jonas sensed confusion and fear. Finally, the child spotted Eliza Jane. He got up and crossed the room to them. "Aunt Liza?"

She reached out to place the backs of her fingers against his cheek in a loving gesture. "Your friends left?"

He nodded, his blue eyes wide and shining. Then so

softly that Jonas could barely hear him, he asked, "Could I sit on your lap for a little while?"

Eliza Jane's composure must've been tested, because she pursed her lips and tilted her head, but recovered and answered swiftly, "Of course you may."

She smoothed the skirts of her black dress, and the boy raised one knee and sidled onto her lap. Her arms came around him, one hand smoothing his hair from his forehead. She pressed a kiss against his temple, and her eyelids drifted closed as though his very scent was a comfort. He snuggled against her.

Jonas's chest got a tight feeling. Her sister's child. When he'd heard the news of Jenny Lee's death in town the day before, he'd also heard clucking and lamenting about the poor dear child and grieving husband she'd left behind. He knew what it was like to lose a mother.

Jonas halted that train of thought. "Your nephew?" he asked.

"This is Tyler. Tyler, meet Mr. Black."

Tyler obediently sat straight and looked at him. "How do, sir."

"Pleased to make your acquaintance, young man."

Tyler looked to Eliza for approval, and she smiled. He tucked himself right back with his head under her chin. "Are you sleepy?" she asked.

"Only a little."

"All this company is tiring, isn't it?"

"Are they all Mama's friends?"

"They came because they cared for her, and they want to show that they care about you, too." She rubbed his shoulder. "Why don't we go upstairs? You can change out of your suit jacket and lie on your bed for a little while."

"I don't want to go yet," he answered.

"All right then. You may sit with me a while longer."

Jonas thought perhaps he should go, but just as he was about to excuse himself, Eliza spoke. "How is Miss Holmes?"

"Good, I reckon. She's a fine worker."

"Housekeeping you said?"

"Uh-huh." Oh, he was a witty conversationalist.

"Do you employ a number of people?"

"About twenty." He explained about the operations of the hotel and the saloon and how many it took to keep both businesses running. "Handle the employment vouchers myself."

"How does that work exactly?"

"Well. You know a lot of men have been lured West by gold or adventure or the dream of land. Reality of it is most of 'em end up needin' jobs. Oh, a few strike it rich and are the moneymakers, but the rest are the real workers. The ones who actually dig trenches and tunnels and drive spikes. Ones who harvest crops and fell trees."

She nodded, showing her interest.

"Those kind of jobs move around with the railroad and with the seasons. Railroad, farmers, mine owners and the state all let me know when they need laborers. I sell vouchers for those jobs and the industry owners pay me commission when they hire."

She didn't respond, and he couldn't read her expression. "I already know your brother-in-law doesn't have any use for what I do."

She glanced away and then back at him. "I don't understand why he calls you a slave trader."

"Maybe he wishes he'd thought of it first?" he suggested with half a grin. "Dunno. They aren't slaves, they're hardworking men. I'm doin' 'em a service by locating the jobs. They call themselves hoboes, you know."

"I didn't. What does that mean?"

"Just means a migratory worker."

"Not tramps."

He shook his head. "Tramps and bums beg and don't want to work. These men are the backbone of industry all the way from here to the Dakotas and up into Canada."

"What about their families?"

"Most of 'em have never been married. Some are immigrants who left wives behind in other countries."

Jonas glanced over and noticed Tyler had fallen asleep in her arms. He was a good-sized boy and must be getting heavy. "He's asleep."

She nodded. "I could tell. He was exhausted. He never sits on my lap anymore. The fact that he did today, not caring who saw, says a lot. Do you think you could help me?"

"What can I do?"

"I don't think I can lift him from where I sit, and I'd never make it up the stairs. I'd hate to wake him to get him to his bed."

Jonas glanced around, not spotting Tyler's father. He stood and bent to take the boy from her arms, getting one arm behind his knees and another around his back. Jonas's arms brushed Eliza Jane's as she released Tyler, and she met his eyes.

Heat like quicksilver ignited in his belly at the combination of that innocent touch and the spark of her amber gaze. *She noticed something, too.*

She stood, smoothing her skirts, and touched his arm. "Upstairs."

She led the way to the foyer and up the broad, carpeted staircase, her black skirts swishing. He glimpsed white lace above her heels with each stair she climbed ahead of him. He didn't allow himself to look up, knowing her backside would be at his eye level.

He followed her along a hallway lined with polished mahogany doors and framed art until she opened one and gestured for him to enter ahead of her. The house smelled like candles and lemon wax.

He carried Tyler into a well-lit room with a heavy oak bedstead and bureau, a chest against one wall, and a row of wooden soldiers at attention along the windowsill.

Eliza Jane tugged at the drapery tassels, letting the material fall over the opening and cloak the room in semidarkness. Moving forward with a rustle of skirts, she pulled back the blue-and-white patterned quilt and a crisp sheet.

Jonas lowered Tyler to the bed, easing his head onto the pillow and straightening his legs.

His aunt removed his boots. Jonas reached to take them from her and set them aside. She pulled the covers up over Tyler and rhythmically threaded her fingers through his hair, as though she was in no hurry to leave him. Jonas couldn't help noticing the pain and adoration on her face when she looked at the boy. She was hurting for him as well as for her own loss.

Bending at the waist, she pressed her nose to his hairline. Her lips touched the skin at his temple. Her eyes closed and Jonas caught the glimmer of a tear as it dropped on Tyler's cheek. She wiped it away quickly and stood. Composing herself she touched her skirt with both hands as though pressing out wrinkles.

He recognized the gesture as something she did without thinking when she was uncomfortable. Following her out into the hall, he stood waiting as she pulled the door closed.

"I'd like to do that myself," she said. "Lie down and obliviously sleep away the next several hours...or days."

"Go ahead."

She looked up at him. The hum of conversation from downstairs seemed to swell and fade. After a second, she shook her head. "The house is full of guests."

"They would understand."

"It's a small thing to honor my sister and let people pay their respects."

He'd been curious about her for months, watching her daily walks to the tea shop, wondering about her life. He suffered a twinge of guilt that perhaps part of his reasoning for coming today had been out of curiosity. It felt odd standing in the home where she had lived for so many years, seeing her in her surroundings, watching her with her nephew. Yet he still didn't know her any better than before.

"This is interesting."

Eliza Jane jumped and turned to face the man who'd spoken.

Royce Dunlap had apparently come up a back flight of stairs and was standing several feet away, looking as though he'd caught them doing something wrong.

Eliza Jane's demeanor changed, her back straightening and chin lifting in a defensive posture. "Mr. Black carried Tyler to his bed. Tyler's had a difficult time and needs to rest."

Royce's gaze slid to Jonas. "Why, how kind of you to assist my son, Jonas. You are a man of many talents. One never knows what you'll be applying yourself to next."

For years Jonas had locked horns with Royce in town council meetings. One discussion or another always led them to a disagreement. Royce had a bone to pick with him for some reason, and Jonas just plain held little respect for the man and his ill treatment of the workers in his employment. But this wasn't the time or the place to air their differences. "I came to show my respects for your wife."

"Yes, we're torn over our loss," Royce replied, but the words and his tone didn't hold much sincerity.

Jonas didn't like the impression he was getting. "I

believe I'll finish my coffee now." He turned to Eliza Jane. "Miss."

"It's probably cold," she told him. "I'll get you a fresh cup."

"No bother. I'll help myself."

Eliza watched his broad back in the black coat as he descended the stairs. She sensed Royce's displeasure and heard him step closer. "He's not our kind, and he's not welcome in this house again."

She frowned, but didn't look at his face. "We don't turn away kind folks who call to pay their respects. He's a perfect gentleman."

"He's a slimy opportunist."

"What are you talking about?" Turning away, she headed for Jenny Lee's room. She and Nora had already cleaned it and replaced all the bedding with new, except for the wedding ring quilt that had been Jenny's favorite. It lay folded over the foot of the bed. The sight made Eliza catch her breath.

She ignored the overwhelming recollections the room stirred up and went directly to the bureau, where she pulled open the second drawer. The wooden box that held Jenny Lee's jewelry was gone. She looked under delicately scented scarves and handkerchiefs that tried to evoke more memories, but there was no jewelry box. Puzzled, she opened and searched each drawer.

Dawning realization kicked her heart into a frantic rhythm. She gave the room a quick once-over and then ran back into the hall.

Royce lounged on a chair that stood alongside a table with a vase. With a smug gaze, he watched her approach.

"Where is Jenny's jewelry box?"

"Why, it's in safekeeping, of course."

"I want to give the jade necklace and earrings to Nora."

He gave a snort of disgust. "Where would that old bag wear jewelry like that?"

Heated anger built in Eliza's chest. "It's of no concern to you where she would wear it or if she wore it at all. It's a gesture of appreciation. Nora cared for Jenny Lee as tenderly as a mother would have. She's like *family* to us. I want to give her a token of some sort. Something sentimental."

"She's not family. She's not anything to us. Jenny Lee's belongings are not yours to disperse."

"That necklace was our mother's. I want Nora to have it."

Royce moved so quickly that Eliza had no warning. Grasping her upper arms, he pushed her against the wall. "Don't defy me, dear sister. Not now. Not ever."

He sidled closer, pressing his thigh between hers.

Eliza struggled to escape, but he raised one hand to her throat and applied enough pressure to cut off her air. "This isn't a game. There are no choices. You're going to marry me. What was Jenny Lee's is mine, and what was yours will be mine."

Her blood pounded in her ears, and she struggled for a much-needed breath. Royce pushed until the bones of her pelvis ached from being pressed between his body and the wall. "Let…go of me," she managed in a hoarse whisper.

He lowered his face close, and she turned hers aside to avoid him. He touched his nose to her cheek. "Don't concern yourself with how I handle things from now on."

Eliza used all her strength to slowly twist sideways, forcing a space between their bodies. When Royce eased away a fraction, she lunged her knee upward between his legs as hard as she could. The contact was swift and solid.

He yelped and released her, doubling over in pain. "You're going to be sorry for that," he said on a groan, but at the moment, his words didn't hold much conviction.

She couldn't shake the descending worry that Jenny Lee's jewelry wasn't the only thing he'd taken. She turned and ran to the end of the hall and up the stairs into the attic. Light streaming in through the arched window at the end of the room allowed her to go directly to the stack of trunks in the corner, where she knelt and reached behind them to grasp blindly.

Her fingers came in contact with the cigar box she'd hidden and relief swept through her in a wave. She'd saved every spare cent she could squirrel away in planning their escape.

As she stood, she realized the box was too light and didn't rattle. She opened it to stare at the bottom. Empty. Her hidden savings were gone. Her means of escape for herself and Tyler…gone.

He'd found it. Royce had deliberately destroyed her plan.

Chapter Five

Eliza trembled with alarming fury and raging fright.

She dropped the cigar box. It landed on the wooden floor with a muffled thud. She stared at the rafters above her head, riding a torrent of fear and panic and regret.

Everything. She'd lost everything. What would she do now? She couldn't stay here. Couldn't live with Royce's constant threats and manipulation. She couldn't bow to his control.

She couldn't marry him, God help her. She *wouldn't*.

Several minutes passed while she pondered her predicament. She owned plenty of assets, including stock in the bank and a portion of the brick company, but she didn't have a nickel she could lay her hands on today or next week or even next month, not without exposing her plan.

How had Royce known about the money? Had he spied on her? Did he search the attic and other rooms on a regular basis? The magnitude of his uncanny power sickened her. Making her way down the narrow stairs and along the hall, she didn't encounter him. She entered her room and washed her face and hands in the tepid water left over from morning. With disgust, she glanced around, imagining him going through her belongings. When did he have time? She was only gone from the house an hour a day.

But he always knew which hour.

After brushing out her hair and collecting it in a fresh chignon, she dabbed glycerin on her hands and face and studied herself in the oval mirror over her washstand. A flush of indignant anger had replaced her pallor and the mounting feelings prompted her to take action.

She wasn't giving up yet.

In his room, Tyler still slept soundly. She tucked the covers around his shoulders and descended the stairs to where townspeople still milled, unaware of the drama being played out behind the scenes in the Sutherland home.

"Nora," she said, finding the woman in the dining room, sponging potato salad from the oval Persian rug. "Put that down and come with me."

Nora handed the sponge and a dish towel to Marian and took the hand Eliza extended.

"Please," Eliza said brightly, leading her toward the wide, open entryway. "I'd like all of you to hear what I have to say." Most of the guests in the parlor and the dining room could hear her from there. The crowd quieted in expectation.

"First I'd like to thank everyone for coming today, and for your prayers and the flowers and food. All of you who knew Jenny Lee know how much she enjoyed being around her friends and family. You were all special to her.

"There are several people who have been especially kind and have given so much of themselves over the years. I'd like to take a minute to thank them." She smoothed her skirt nervously, but pressed on. "Most of you remember Dr. Black. He was a godsend to the Sutherlands. I still miss him as I'm sure many of you do."

Neighbors nodded in agreement.

Her gaze found Jonas standing beside George Atwell. Jonas nodded in recognition.

"More recently," she continued, "over the past couple of years, Dr. McKee was Jenny's doctor. She trusted him, and he did all he could to make her more comfortable. Dr. McKee, you have a kind heart."

Hands in pockets, Kerwin McKee looked at his shoes. The man next to him nudged his shoulder.

"I'd like you to have my father's desk set," Eliza told him. "It's carved teakwood and there's a humidor and some other pieces that can sit on your office desk."

"No call for that, Miss Eliza Jane," the doctor said.

"No argument. Jenny would want you to have it," Eliza told him. "So do I."

Continuing, Eliza turned to her friend. "You all probably know what a godsend Nora has been to my family. She was always here for my mother. She helped Jenny and me through our father's illness. I couldn't have made it through without her. There's no way to say thank you for such selflessness."

Tears welled up in Nora's eyes. Her husband came and stood beside her and put his arm around her waist. "Your mama was my dearest friend," she said with a sniffle, and took a hankie from her pocket to dab her nose. "She would have been so proud of you."

Eliza ignored the emotions that tried to undermine her purpose. She had to save herself and Tyler, and she was going to do it right. "I have a little something for you, too, Nora. Just so you know how much you are loved by the Sutherlands."

Eliza walked several feet into the hallway, and a few people moved aside to make way for her. She reached up and took the Horace Vernet painting from where it hung on a cord from the crown molding and carried it to Nora. "You always admired this. We want you to have it."

The observers murmured and a few whispered.

Nora looked at Eliza with surprise, but genuine pleasure touched her wary features. "What a generous gift!" she said with a tearful smile. "I never dreamed to own something so lovely."

"Well, it's yours." Eliza glanced at the nearby faces, seeing smiles and a few tears. Her gaze moved unerringly until she found Royce standing stiffly near the dining room doorway. He wore a fierce scowl, and his neck was brick-red against the white collar of his starched shirt. She remembered his hand at her throat and his smug pleasure at robbing her. She could still do something to save herself.

"Since rumors spread so quickly," she said, deliberately allowing her gaze to linger on her brother-in-law for a moment before looking away. "I'd like all of you to hear this firsthand. Tyler and I will be going to stay at the hotel temporarily. My sister is no longer here, and Nora won't be at the house daily. It would be inappropriate for my brother-in-law and I to live under the same roof without a chaperone.

"I don't wish to burden my brother-in-law with domestic concerns, so Tyler will attend school as usual and I will care for him as always.

"We haven't had time to make any definite plans or sort things out, and… Well, the truth is, I need some time away from this place where all my memories are so fresh." Eliza didn't have to fake the tremor of emotion that wavered in her voice.

"Of course you do, dear," Miss Fletcher said. "You'll have plenty of time to decide what to do after the two of you have observed a mourning period."

Eliza nodded, and with quiet words of encouragement, the other guests agreed.

Edward Phillips, the banker, turned to Royce and laid a hand on his shoulder. Royce drew his ominous stare from Eliza, and Luther Vernon blocked her view.

She had never been sure what position Luther held to earn his place on Sutherland Brick's payroll. He never dressed like a factory worker and most often accompanied Royce. But all of her questions about the operations of the business had been met with contemptuous instructions to stay out of Royce's way.

She'd won this hand. She'd bought herself a couple of months at the most. Royce couldn't defy her public decision to observe propriety, but he would be biding his time until the allotted weeks of mourning had passed. And then he would play his trump card. By then Eliza needed to have a better plan. There was still time to set aside some cash for train fare and travel— if she could get a job.

There was one person she could ask to help her find a job and keep it a secret from Royce. Her gaze sought and found him. He appeared to be listening to Reverend Miller, but his awareness was focused on her.

She was placing her last hope on Jonas Black.

Jonas paused in the hallway. A torrent of complaints, punctuated by the clattering of pots and pans, streamed from the kitchen at the back of the hotel on the ground floor.

"Told ya she's been howlin' like that for half an hour," Quay told him. "Phoebe came and got me, but I barely got m' head inside the door afore she started throwing skillets."

Jonas glanced at the massive door, wishing he could just leave until the storm passed. He had to be the one to assuage Lilibelle's temper however. "I've got this. You go check in the delivery that's pulling up in the alley."

"Thanks, boss." Quay lit out before Jonas could say another word.

Jonas glanced at his pocket watch, relieved that

breakfast guests were well on their way for the day and there were no guests in the foyer or dining room. He strode along the polished oak floors until he reached the kitchen door. After only a momentary pause, he pushed it open.

"What's all the racket about, Lily? You've sent the girls runnin' for cover. Is it your intent to chase off the kitchen help?"

"It's my intent to prepare salmon steaks with mustard sauce for supper this evening, but I can't make salmon steaks if I don't have salmon!" Lilibelle gestured wildly with the wooden spoon she held. The starched white apron that covered her ample bosom and rounded belly drew attention to the fact that not only was she twice the size of any other person who worked in the kitchen, but twice as clean. Lilibelle Grimshaw cooked for the hotel dining room, and she was a stickler for setting and following rules, and that included menu plans.

"I do see your dilemma," Jonas said with all seriousness. "That would be the recipe with parsley and butter I like so well?"

"The *very* one!" She struck the spoon against the cast-iron stove and it shot out of her hold to flip in the air and clatter on the smooth oak floor. "The train's come and gone and Pool tells me they didn't bring the salmon. I sent him off to the telegraph office with a piece of my mind."

"Well, the supplier deserves that, if not worse for disappointin' you." Jonas walked around the long work-table that separated him from the cook and stooped to pick up a kettle, then glanced at the open back door and the crates outside. "What *did* they deliver?"

"Duck!" she shouted and slammed a skillet on the worktable.

"I guess duck is a lot more difficult to prepare than salmon," he said, as though wondering.

"Duck needs to be roasted slowly," she replied, then turned to pick up a white towel and dab her red face with the damp corners.

"How do you make that sauce that goes on it?"

"With grated orange peel and wine, a little Worcestershire and cayenne. It's not all that tough."

"That's sounding awfully tasty to be truthful. And your rice always turns out just right."

She picked up the wooden spoon from the floor with a grunt and mumbled.

"I'm thinking duck would be a good choice for this evenin'," he told her. "You can make salmon once that incompetent warehouse puts your order together correctly. I'll handle that myself."

"They should reduce the cost for the inconvenience," she said with a haughty flick of her pudgy fingers.

"I'll see that they do."

"Get on about your day then, and let me get to work on dinner," she told him. "Where are those silly girls who are supposed to be peeling apples?"

"I do believe you scared 'em all away, Lily. Remember some of these girls have been boxed around a mite. They take to cover when tempers flare and things start flyin'." He fixed her with a square look.

She acquiesced to his wisdom with a quick nod and a grimace. "If you see the shrinking violets out there, tell 'em I'm not going to bite their heads off," she replied.

"I'll tell 'em." Jonas skirted the back hall and dining room, finding Yvonne and Nadine folding napkins and making themselves as small as possible. "Apologies for that," he said, jerking a thumb over his shoulder. "She's calmed down now. Give her a couple more minutes and then act like nothin' ever happened. You okay?"

Both women nodded, and Jonas offered them an apologetic nod before grabbing his hat and heading for the door.

In the wide foyer, a woman stood at the front desk, a stack of colorful hatboxes at her feet. His heart recognized Eliza Jane with a burst of pumping blood before his eyes registered the fact with his brain. "Miss Sutherland?"

She turned. "Good morning."

"Didn't expect you so soon." Her sister's funeral had only been the day before.

She glanced at Ward, the man who handled the desk and guests. He had filled out a few lines in the registry book, and then turned to search for a key. "I'm prone to facing what needs to be done," she said.

"We have somethin' in common then. How's Tyler?"

"He was quiet this morning. He wanted to go to school, and I saw no reason to hold him out if he was up to it."

"Takes after you by gettin' on with things."

"Perhaps."

"Let me help you with the rest of your things."

"There's a wagon out front," she told him.

"Are there a couple of strong men aboard?" he asked with a grin.

"I often travel with several strong men at a time," she replied, "but today I brought only one. Will he do?"

"Reckon that depends on the size of your trunks."

"My trunks have been known to make grown men cry," she told him. "Perhaps you'll want to send for reinforcements."

His gaze went from her twinkling eyes to Ward, who by now was dangling the room key above the counter.

"You go open the door to room…" Jonas paused.

"Twenty," Ward replied.

"Room twenty," Jonas repeated, "and I'll do my best not to cry."

She smiled, apparently amused with their banter. "I shall be waiting. On which floor will I find room twenty?"

"The third," Ward and Jonas said at the same time.

"I'm sure I'll enjoy the view," she added.

Jonas headed outside. Indeed, if six trunks were any indication, she'd brought enough to stay several weeks, if not months. He eyeballed the smallest one, thinking to warm up to the largest, but the lad who'd been waiting on the curb jumped into the back of the wagon and drew that particular piece of luggage toward him.

"Third floor," Jonas told the young man, then wrestled a trunk onto his shoulder.

By the time they'd both made two trips, they looked

at each other, and in silent agreement, each took a handle and shared the weight.

"One more," he said to Eliza Jane on the way out of the room again, trying not to wheeze as he said it.

He and the driver of the wagon looked at each other again. "Last one," Jonas said.

"The last," the boy agreed. Perspiration shone on his upper lip. They had to set down the trunk on the first landing to catch their breath. Then again at the top of the stairs. Both put on their poker faces and carried their burden into Eliza Jane's room as though it was the first.

She handed the boy several coins and thanked him. He left with a sideways look at Jonas, leaving the door standing open.

She'd rented one of the larger rooms, one with two beds and a sitting area, a gateleg table and writing desk. A braided rug and two chairs sat before a brick fireplace.

"I never knew what a nice hotel you owned here," she told him. "I've eaten in the dining room, of course, but I've never seen the rooms."

"They're not all this grand. You asked for a big one."

"I put the bill on the company tab."

"No problem there." He started for the door. "I'll leave you to your unpackin'. If you have need of anythin', just let Ward know."

"Jonas."

He liked the sound of his name when she said it. He stopped and turned back. "Miss?"

"I'd like to speak with you. Please."

The door was still open to the hall behind him. If anyone passed in the hallway, there would be no speculation. "What is it?"

She took off her straw hat and looked for a place to set it. She found a peg just inside the door, but hanging it brought her closer to where he stood.

Her hair was black and shiny, and today she wore it in a loose knot, with a curling length hanging down her back. She'd somehow nestled in a nosegay of tiny pastel paper flowers. Foolish of him to notice such a feminine detail.

"Is there a position I could fill while I'm staying here?"

"A position?" he asked.

"A job."

It was common knowledge that she'd worked at Sutherland Brick Company for a good many years until she resigned to care for her sister. Her family owned the company, along with a fair amount of real estate in this town. Why would she ask *him* for a job? "What about the factory?"

"What about it?"

"I just figured if you wanted to work, you could go back to your job there. Or make another place for yourself."

"I won't be working at the factory," she told him. His expression must have shown his confusion, because she added, "It's complicated. I'll take any work you have for me. I can cook, clean, change bedding."

"Just doesn't seem like the work you're used to."

"On the contrary." She rubbed her palms on her skirt and added quickly, "All I've done for months is cook and clean and change bedding. I'm up to the task."

"Most of the women here were down on their luck when they arrived. They're not...what you're used to."

She straightened her shoulders. "Do you imagine I hold myself in higher regard than your employees? I assure you I will not cause a problem."

"Didn't think you would."

"If you won't hire me, then sell me a voucher. I'll go work for someone else."

"There's nothin' local to be had. Jobs are in other states most o' the time."

She appeared a trifle unsure if the wrinkle in her brow was any indication. "I must have an income. I'll have to find work somewhere else if you won't help me."

Her amber eyes were lit with conviction. But why would she take her nephew to an unfamiliar place when she had a home and business right here? "Don't get upset," he told her. "I've already dealt with one emotional woman today. If you're willin' to work for the same pay as the other housekeepers, I can put you to work first thing in the mornin'."

"I am," she said quickly.

"You'd follow directions from Ada Harper, and she'd let you know where to start. Mostly laundry and room cleanin', if that suits you."

"That's suits me just fine. Thank you."

"All right then. Breakfast and lunch are set out in the

kitchen. Help yourself and have a seat at the north end of the dining room. Put a tally on the chalkboard for prepared box lunches for the young'un. You and the boy are welcome to take your meals in the dining room of an evenin', as well. Employees mostly gather on the north end then, too, but there's no rule."

"One more thing," she added.

He waited without speaking.

She clasped her hands together and raised her chin to look him in the eye. "I don't want my brother-in-law to know I'm working here. He…he wouldn't understand my need to keep busy."

Now the situation seemed really fishy. She wanted a job, and she didn't want Royce Dunlap to know about it. The whole thing didn't sit right with Jonas, but her earnest expression told him how important this was to her. Something in the soft vulnerability of her mouth and the way she held herself in a show of bravado spoke to a place of less resistance inside him. He behaved uncharacteristically around her, so he'd darned well better watch what he was getting himself into.

"Can it be just between us?" she pressed. "I'm not asking you to swear your other employees to secrecy. I doubt they'd have any call to mention it to someone who'd leak it back to Royce, anyway. I just need a few weeks. *Please*."

It was the *please* that did it. Breathless and almost intimate in the way she spoke it. "I won't have call to talk to him about it," he answered finally.

"Thank you."

Her relief was obvious in the way the tension left her body and in the light that sparkled from her eyes. They were the rich color of pure sweet honey. Helping this woman affected him more than it should have. Considering how out of kilter she made him feel, his gut reactions were downright dangerous.

Hoping he wasn't going to regret any of this, he headed for the door. The woman already had him asking mental questions and keepin' secrets. What in tarnation was comin' next? "You're welcome," he said. "I think."

Chapter Six

Eliza listened to the sound of Tyler's breathing well into the darkest hours. The bed in which she was lying was comfortable, the linens smelling of fresh air and castile soap. It was a fair night, and a soft, cool breeze wafted through the partially open window, rustling the cotton print curtains and caressing the skin of her face and arms. There was nothing about the conditions of the room or the weather to prevent her from sleeping, but she was wide-awake just the same.

Perhaps this vague unfamiliar restlessness was a result of the tiny measure of freedom she'd been granted. For the first time in months, she felt as though she could take a deep breath. Their time spent here was only a brief reprieve, but a buoyant hope surfaced anyway.

She'd only slept away from the house on Walnut Street a few times in her entire life, and those nights had been during trips with her parents, and in later years with Jenny Lee. Being completely alone with Tyler, completely responsible for his future and well-being was frightening. But her love for him gave her courage to do anything, even make difficult choices and defy the man who wanted to control their lives.

Royce didn't care for Tyler any more than he'd ever cared for Jenny. Nor was there anything more than greed and manipulation fueling the advances he made toward Eliza. If he wanted her, it was only because of the financial control and power that possessing her would bring him. A chill shuddered along her bare arms and skittered across her shoulders at the thought of her brother-in-law's lurid expectations.

Eliza tossed off the covers and stood, pulling on her cotton wrapper, which had been lying across the foot of the bed. Silently, she padded across the room to the window and pushed aside the curtain to peer out at the night.

The muted sounds from the saloon had ceased an hour or more ago, and the warm night lay silent. The western sky was bright with stars, and the scent of sage was on the breeze. Thinking it might get cooler as the night deepened, she pulled the window closed. After she found her slippers in the bottom of the armoire, she stole out of the room, locking the door for Tyler's safety, and dropping the key into her pocket.

She made her way along the hallway and down the stairs to cross the empty lobby, which was lit by a dimly burning oil lamp on the wall. Remembering the row of cushioned wicker chairs across the porch, she slipped out the front door and stood at the porch railing, gazing out at the silent street and the expanse of dark sky.

As young girls, she and Jenny had often made pallets on their front porch and spent carefree summer nights speculating about the stars and their futures. Eliza had ruined her own future years ago, and Jenny had made the mistake of falling for Royce's slick charm. Her chest ached with regret and sadness for their broken dreams.

Back then she'd never envisioned a future without Jenny. A wave of panic washed over her at the responsibility she now held, and she placed her fingers over her lips.

"Somethin' wrong, Miss Sutherland?"

At the deep voice behind her, Eliza spun to face Jonas. Her heart pounded against her ribs. "No," she answered, taking a few deep breaths to calm herself. "I couldn't sleep is all."

"Is your room sufficient?"

"Yes, of course. It's quite nice, actually. I'm just… having some trouble making adjustments."

He moved to the railing and leaned back until he sat with one thigh crooked atop the rail, the other foot on the porch floor. "Like losin' your sister?"

She held the front of her wrapper together under her chin. "Mostly."

"I never did know what caused her to be sickly."

"She had scarlet fever when she was a child. Your father and the other doctors believed it weakened her heart."

"It's a wonder, isn't it, how some folks go their whole lives with everythin' falling into place, while others have to face double the hardship? Kind of makes a body wonder how it all evens out in the end...or if it ever does."

A deep thought from a man who appeared so rough around the edges. Was he referring to her or to himself? She wasn't comfortable asking.

He shrugged then, as if he didn't know either way.

She sensed an underlying current in the air...something he wasn't saying...something she wasn't admitting. "All we know about most people is what they let us see," she said finally.

"Unless we dig deeper," he answered. "Or get to know 'em better."

He'd managed to surprise her again. "Are you a philosopher?"

He chuckled.

The sound put her at ease for the first time in days.

"Everybody who's spent enough nights around a campfire is a philosopher," he answered.

"How many campfires have you seen?"

"I spent my youth drivin' cattle, playin' cards, listenin' to the old-timers. Did my time in the army after that."

"You always seemed very mysterious," she admitted. "When you arrived in Silver Bend after all those years, stories were tossed about. There was speculation. Some said you and your father never got along. Others said you had a wild wandering spirit you had to satisfy."

"Are you digging deeper?" he asked.

"If I am, are you going to let me see another side of you?"

The words were far bolder than she'd intended. Her cheeks grew warm, and she was glad for the cover of night.

"I left when I was thirteen because I couldn't stand to watch my father drink himself into a stupor every night."

Surprised at his straightforward admission, Eliza turned to face him. "I heard talk about his drinking," she told him. "But I didn't know whether or not to believe it."

"Believe it."

"It never affected the care he gave my mother or my sister."

"He was always good at doctorin'," he said with a nod. "Not so good at fathering. He had so much remorse festerin' inside, he couldn't get on with life."

"I'm surprised," she told him, forced now to wonder about the man she'd seen so often, yet apparently hadn't known all that well.

"That I said it or that it could be true?"

"I don't doubt it's true. I have no reason to question you. I'm surprised that it's a fact. I had no idea."

"We all have things in our pasts we don't take out and kick around," he said. "Wouldn't do much good if we did."

He was right about that. What was done was done.

She stepped toward the railing where he sat, and glanced upward into the vast expanse of black sky and spotted the hazy yellow moon.

"So, you wondered about me?" he asked. "When others were talkin'?"

"Some."

"I wondered about you," he told her. "Wondered why you walk into town every day at the same time."

"I went for tea."

"I know. But why?"

"My sister insisted I have a little time to myself every day."

"You took care of her for a long time."

"Yes."

"Never got married."

"Are you pointing out the fact or asking why? Weren't the reasons apparent?"

"Wasn't an accusation," he said quietly. "Just an observation."

"Do people talk about my lack of a husband, or is that your own curiosity?"

"Reckon I'm curious. You're from a good family. Smart. More'n pretty enough."

At the combination of his words and the way he looked at her, her cheeks grew warm again.

"My guess is you've set your sights a mite too high."

She had to laugh at that thought. "The fact is, I've been too busy to meet men, other than those my brother-in-law brings home for dinner occasionally, and most of them are married."

"Wasn't always like that, was it?" He reached for her hand and held it. "I mean before Jenny Lee got so sick, back when you worked at the brickyard? There were probably beaus callin' on you then."

His gentle touch broke down more barriers. "Maybe one or two."

"Now we're gettin' somewhere."

She succumbed to his teasing voice. The cover of night and his persuasive voice coaxed feelings and words into the open. "There was one special someone once."

His thumb stroked the back of her hand, and sent a delicious tingle up her arm. "What was his name?"

She hadn't said the name aloud in years. The prospect of doing so now made her stomach feel as if she was teetering on the edge of a cliff. "Forest," she managed. "My father didn't have any sons, and he was quite fond of Forest. He took him under his wing and taught him the business."

"I thought Royce was his protégé."

"Royce was his second choice," she said, the fact giving her petty satisfaction. "I had an aptitude with numbers, so I was Father's bookkeeper. It was while I was handling accounts and initiating investments that we became railroad and bank shareholders."

"Impressive."

"Not to my father. He turned his favor on the young men. First Forest and then Royce."

"Did you love Forest?"

Deeply buried hurts unfolded inside her. "I thought I did."

"What happened?"

It seemed natural to turn her hand and grasp his hand in return, the gesture like an unspoken trust between them. "He left town without warning. Just…disappeared and was gone."

Her father had blamed her for running him off, but

she didn't tell Jonas that. All of it hurt, but taking the blame for her father losing his protégé still rankled. She didn't know what she'd done wrong, unless giving her heart had been a mistake.

"I always wondered if I'd ever see him again, but Silver Bend is just a drop in the world that's out there beyond Montana. He could be anywhere."

"Man was a damned fool," Jonas said with enough conviction to bring tears to her eyes. He must have noticed her reaction, because he tugged, and she let him draw her closer, right up until her thigh brushed his and he put his other arm around her waist.

Due to his sitting position on the railing, his face was lower than hers by a few inches. With his warm palm flattened against her back, he drew her even closer, releasing her hand so he could envelop her in his warmth and strength. She didn't resist, didn't even want to. At the feel of his strong arms around her, silken pearls of fire rolled along her nerve endings and spread throughout her body. The liberating sensation was like a promise she'd been waiting to fulfill.

She had no reason on earth to deny herself this pleasure, nothing more to lose, so she met his kiss, threading her fingers into his soft cool hair at the same time she tasted his lips.

She savored the warmth of his mouth, loved the feel of his hands on her waist, sliding to her hips, as he took control of the kiss and stood to tuck her tightly against his length. Eliza was starving for affection, for attention…for someone to recognize and want her for who she was. Her neediness almost embarrassed her, but she didn't care. This was her moment. Her tiny dash at satisfaction, and she meant to grab it.

A shot rang through the air. A thud sounded and Jonas's body jerked at the same time he gasped against her mouth. In the next instant as wood splintered overhead, he grabbed her and pushed her to the porch floor, lying with his hard body covering her. Her heart pounded so loud she could barely hear his breathing.

He leaned to one side, unpinning her. "Crawl to the door and get inside."

The night was eerily silent. Nothing moved or rustled. She wanted to obey, but couldn't make herself budge.

Behind them, the wooden screen covering the parlor window creaked open a few inches and a dark object fell to the porch floor with a thud.

Jonas inched backward, grabbed the leather holster with his left hand and drew out a long revolver. "Inside *now*," he said to her.

In the moonlight, a dark patch glistened high on the white sleeve of his shirt on his right side.

"You're hurt."

"Can't feel it yet," he told her. "Now get in. Keep everyone away from the windows."

Crawling was awkward until she hiked her nightdress and wrapper above her knees. He remained beside her, reaching for the door handle and closing her safely inside.

Jonas peered around the pillar. The post wasn't much

cover, but the lack of bright moonlight aided him in staying in the shadows. He waited several minutes, but couldn't make out anything unusual in the gray shapes along the street. The shot had most likely come from between buildings on the other side.

He leaped over the porch railing on the west and crouched as he ran between the hotel and the dry goods store to the back alley. The store was on the corner of the block. Because of the cover, the shooter would expect him to take the alley eastward and then get to the other side somewhere near the saloon.

Instead, he crossed the street to the west and ran the entire length of the alley to come out farther down. He approached the boardwalk in a crouch, wondering as the numbness left his good arm by increments, if he'd be able to hit anything.

At some point he still had to get across Main, so he made a run for it, then worked his way behind the south-side buildings.

"Who's out there?"

Jonas recognized Yale Baxter, who lived above his hardware store on the corner. Yale was wearing his union suit and carrying a Winchester. Jonas answered in a low voice. "Jonas. Somebody was shooting at the hotel."

"Anybody hurt?"

"Got a slug in my shoulder that's startin' to hurt like the very devil."

Across the street beside the tea shop loomed two more residents carrying guns. "Yale? Jonas, that you?

Jonas called a low reply. George Atwell and Marshal

Haglar crossed the street, George wearing trousers with suspenders over his bare shoulders and Warren fully dressed as though he hadn't been to bed yet.

"Somebody shot Jonas," Yale told them.

"The hell. We been up and down the alley on this side," Warren answered. "Whoever it was is long gone."

"Or back inside," George added.

"Who'd want to shoot you?" Warren asked.

"I made that Baslow fella pretty mad," he replied.

"I checked on him a week ago, and he was on his ranch where he's supposed to be," Warren said.

"Let's get ya to Doc's." Yale gestured with the rifle barrel. "Get ya stitched up." He walked around Jonas, squinting in the moonlight. "Can't see blood in the back."

Jonas headed east on the boardwalk. "Great."

A few neighbors were gathered in front of the hotel, a couple carrying lanterns and most with rifles.

Lilibelle and the other women were gathered on the hotel porch, and Jonas recognized Bonnie Jacobson in her flannel nightdress and shawl, walking toward him. "Dr. McKee is waiting for you."

Yale accompanied Jonas to Doc's, which was another block's walk. As soon as the small square frame house came into view, Jonas's stomach clenched. Damned if he wouldn't have to go inside.

"Gonna pass out on me?" Yale asked.

Jonas straightened and drew a sustaining breath. He could do it. He could walk in there and not see the blood or hear the cries that were a part of his darkest memories. He wasn't ten years old. "I'm all right."

Etta McKee had painted the plaster walls yellow and hung checkered curtains on every window. The house looked nothing like it did in Jonas's nightmares.

The examining room was just as he remembered. The walls were lined with wood cabinets, and glass jars filled with utensils sat on every surface.

"Let's see what we got here." Kerwin put on his spectacles. His wiry brown hair stuck up on one side as though he'd just climbed out of bed. He cut off Jonas's shirt. "Slug's still in there."

Etta hurried in with a half-full bottle of whiskey and a small glass. She poured a generous amount and set it on the worktable with a solid thud.

"Jonas don't drink," Yale told her, then picked up the glass and downed the contents.

Jonas took a seat on a sturdy chair. "Get to it."

He closed his eyes and resolutely thought about those fleeting moments with Eliza Jane before bullets had started flying.

Yale moved to sit in the outer room in his union suit, drinking Etta's coffee while Jonas cursed through clenched teeth. Forty minutes and a couple hundred inventive swearwords later, Jonas walked out of the examining room with his bare shoulder bandaged and his arm in a sling. He acknowledged the doctor's missus with a nod. "Pardon, ma'am."

She waved a hand. "I was along when Laura Brinkley gave birth to twins last week. Now that woman's cursing could strip the bark from trees. You get some rest."

"Yes, ma'am."

Everyone had gone back to his or her beds, and the dark street was quiet, save for the sound of their boot heels on the boardwalks. Thunder rumbled across the heavens.

"We got here just in time," Yale said.

Jonas was a mite unsteady on his feet the last several yards to the hotel. Just as the first rain pelted their heads and shoulders, Yale supported him and helped him onto the porch.

Eliza was perched on the stairs inside, waiting, with Lilibelle seated on a chair she'd brought from the dining room. "Did your boy sleep through the commotion?" Lilibelle asked.

"I checked on him twice to be certain. Tyler can sleep through anything."

At the sound of boots on the porch, Eliza got up and hurried forward, while Lily took a little more time getting to her feet.

Looking unusually pale, Jonas was leaning heavily on another man as the two of them lunged across the threshold.

"He's gonna be fine," the other man told them. "Doc dug out a slug."

"Walk him on up to his rooms, Mr. Baxter," Lily said. "Lead the way, Eliza Jane. I'm not climbing those stairs again tonight."

Eliza had helped Lily and Phoebe prepare the bed with additional layers of sheets. They'd warmed water for washing. His quarters took up one entire end of the second floor and consisted of a large sitting room and a separate sleeping area. The furnishings were dark heavy wood, solid, but not elaborate.

Eliza opened the door and stood just inside as the man in his union suit entered behind Jonas.

"I'm all right." Jonas's skin appeared dark against the white bandages.

"Take that elixir the doc gave you," Baxter told him.

Jonas nodded, and the man left.

"There's warm water," Eliza said.

He placed his revolver on the bureau and met her gaze in the framed mirror. "You all right?"

"Perfectly." She moved forward. "Let me help you." She took the washrag, soaked it and wrung it in the basin. Streaks of blood had dried on his arm, and she wiped them away gently with the wet cloth. "I heard you didn't find anyone."

"He got away."

"Has anything like this ever happened before? Do you have any idea who it might have been?"

"First thought was Baslow," he said.

She'd considered him, too. The man had been furious with Jonas.

"Do you want to wash your face?"

He nodded.

She soaped the cloth and handed it to him. After he washed, she rinsed it out and gave it back. He gave his skin a halfhearted swipe.

"Here," she said, taking the cloth and wiping his face. He closed his eyes. Standing close, reaching up to perform the task, her breast brushed the back of his fingers where they protruded from the sling.

His eyes opened and his dark gaze burned into hers. A sensation like heat lightning skittered through her body. Their kiss was foremost in her thoughts, but she suspected Jonas had more significant things on his mind.

A flash of lightning lit the end of the room, followed by the low rumble of thunder. She busied herself drying him with the towel. Sweat had already broken out on his forehead. "Where's the medicine?" she asked.

He reached into his left pocket with his good hand and drew out a slim brown bottle. "A teaspoonful."

"I'll get a spoon." She hurried downstairs and fumbled her way into the dark kitchen to retrieve the utensil. The rain beat a rhythm on the tin stovepipe as she searched drawers and cupboards. When she returned, he was lying on his back on the bed, one booted foot crossed over the other, mouth in a grim line.

She measured the dose.

"I'll do it." He sat up and took the spoon from her, their fingers brushing. A drip hit his trousers during the transfer.

She capped the bottle and set it away. "Let me help you get your boots off."

He offered one leg at a time, and she tugged until they slid off. Uncomfortable now, she wondered if he wanted to strip out of his trousers. "I can get someone else to help with the rest."

"I can undress myself," he assured her. "C'mere first."

She took a hesitant step closer to the edge of his bed. He reclined and closed his eyes, but not until he'd reached for her hand and she allowed him to hold it. "You need to rest," she told him.

"Tell me now if you're gonna pretend like nothin' ever happened, so I'll know what to expect."

It took her a minute to collect her thoughts.

"I don't think I could pretend that well," she replied at last. Whatever happened next, that tantalizing kiss—and his warm embrace—would be with her forever.

He opened his eyes to look at her then. "That's good to know."

She should have told him right then and there that anything more between them would be impossible. He needed to know she wasn't sticking around any longer than it took to earn traveling money. But it was late, and he was hurting and needed his rest. Her bubble of self-delusion would burst soon enough. Until reality was once again her closest companion, she had this briefest of hours to dream.

And she didn't want to forget that kiss.

Chapter Seven

Ada Harper had worked at the hotel since its construction, Eliza learned the next morning. She shared that she'd had a husband once, but he'd deserted her and their two small children five years ago. After she eked out a living in a mining camp that was eventually abandoned, her last coins had brought her this far. She'd been ready to foster out her children to spare them starvation when Jonas had hired her. Her family now lived in a sturdy little house and owned a cow and half a dozen chickens.

"My boys go to school and then hire out to the ranchers in the fall," she told Eliza. "Fine young men they're growing up to be."

Eliza and Tyler had met her sons Matt and Daniel at supper the evening before. They were polite young fellows of eleven and thirteen who spoke respectfully to their mother and kindly to Tyler. Ada's story gave Eliza hope that a woman alone could raise a boy and do well

by him. Of course—and this gave her pause for regret—
she was running from the very place and the man that
had been Ada's deliverance.

She enjoyed tucking clean sheets around the mat-
tresses, dusting rooms and polishing furniture that day.
Though the tasks were simple, she was keeping busy
and earning a wage. Checking her brooch at three
o'clock, she wondered if Bonnie would miss her afternoon visit. Eliza had neglected to mention to Ada that
she would be walking to school to collect Tyler. After
looking, she couldn't locate the woman. She asked
Ward where she might find Jonas.

"At his office down at the saloon, miss."

She had time, so she freshened up and pulled on her
bonnet before strolling eastward four doors to the Silver
Star. The green enamel batwing doors were hooked
open against the exterior wall, and two mahogany-
stained doors stood closed against the afternoon sun.
Eliza Jane opened one and entered. She'd never been
inside the Silver Star Saloon. Before Jonas had purchased and renovated the business, it had been a disrep-
utable hangout, populated by drifters and no-accounts
who occasionally shot up Main Street and often mistreated the women of ill repute who worked there.

No sign of the past remained now as she studied the
interior. Sun streaked through sparkling clean windows
and louvered shutters, creating interesting blocks of
light on the clean, polished oak floor. Three men sat eating at a table, and a couple others were playing cards
at the back of the room.

She'd heard how Jonas had gutted the interior and designed it to welcome respectable clientele. There were ladies in town who still believed any establishment that sold liquor was scandalous, but the town council appreciated the taxes the profitable business paid into the coffers.

The tall, slender man standing behind the bar greeted Eliza. "Afternoon, miss. What can I get for you?"

"I came to speak with Mr. Black."

The man walked to the open end of the bar and pointed down a corridor. "Second door back there."

She thanked him, traveled the hall to where he'd shown her and knocked lightly.

"C'mon in."

She opened the door. Jonas stood at a window, dressed as usual in dark trousers and a light blue shirt. He was holding the arm that rested in the sling with the opposite hand. She noted there wasn't much of a view, what with a brick building next door.

He turned. "Eliza Jane? Somethin' wrong?"

"No. Nothing. I forgot to mention to Mrs. Harper that I'd need to leave long enough to fetch Tyler from school. I didn't find her anywhere."

"Go," he told her. His hair looked as though he'd run his hand through it half-a-dozen times, and his expression was hard.

"Is your arm hurting?" she asked.

"Like a—" He bit off whatever he'd been about to say and nodded. "Doc came by. Said I have a fever. Warned me to rest."

"You should be in bed then."

He scowled at the pile of papers and the open ledger on his desk. "Too much work to be done."

"Won't it wait a few days?"

He shook his head. "Payroll needs to be figured. And there's a mix-up with a couple of deliveries."

She glanced at the ledger. "I could do it for you."

"The payroll?"

She nodded. "I'm quite efficient, actually. Would you like me to look it over?"

He hesitated a moment, but then nodded. "Reckon you've figured plenty of payroll accounts, eh?"

"Reckon I have," she replied with a grin.

One side of his mouth curled up at her teasing. "Go get your nephew. After today the Harper boys can gather him and walk him home. If that suits you."

"Tyler has been acting embarrassed that I come to walk him home," she admitted. "I think he'd like being with the older boys."

"Go on and get him. Tell Ada you'll be helpin' me here. Ask Matt and Danny to look after Tyler until supper. He can help them with their chores."

"Is it safe?" she asked.

"Lily's bark is louder'n her bite. They'll fetch her wood and pump water. She'll sneak 'em cookies."

Assured, she headed for the door, glancing back. "Did you take the medicine?"

"Makes me too sleepy. I'll take it tonight."

Eliza left the Silver Star and headed back along Main past the hotel. From across the street, Bonnie opened her door and called out, "Afternoon, Eliza Jane! I missed you today."

Eliza glanced at the street before running across. "I probably won't be in to have tea for a while."

She didn't feel she should try to explain. Anything she said would sound awkward. She didn't want to lie, but she couldn't tell Bonnie she was working.

"Well, stop whenever you can," Bonnie offered.

"I will, thanks." Another block and she crossed to the grassy area where the school was situated. The children were already trailing from the building, and Tyler spotted her immediately.

"Jimmy Jeffries brought a snake in a big jar today," he told her.

"Oh my goodness."

"It had yellow stripes. Danny said it's a wandering garter snake and he says maybe *we* can find us one!"

The Harper boys were walking a few feet behind them, so Eliza turned to include them in their conversation.

"There's tall grass 'cross the alley behind the dry goods store," Danny said. "Snakes're in there for sure."

"Do you know the difference between the safe snakes and dangerous ones?" Eliza asked.

"Yup," Matt replied importantly. "Jonas showed us a long while ago when he found out we played back there sometimes."

Eliza nodded, still not certain snake hunting sounded like a safe pastime.

She shared what Jonas had said about looking after

Tyler, and watched them enter the hotel before continuing on to the saloon.

Jonas was seated on a chair at the table with the card players when she arrived. He stood and accompanied her to his office. "Been thinkin' to take this stuff to the hotel, so you can work there."

"Whatever you prefer."

"More people are likely to see you comin' here is all. What with you wanting to keep your employment a secret, I thought it'd be wiser."

"I appreciate that."

Jonas's entire arm throbbed, all the way from his shoulder to his wrist. The more tasks he couldn't do and the fiercer the wound hurt, the more frustrated he'd grown throughout the day. Though it galled him to admit he needed it, Eliza Jane's help would make a big difference. "Tyler all right?"

Tyler hadn't mentioned Jenny. Hadn't mentioned going to the house or seeing Royce. "He's pleased to have a change, and the Harper boys are older and exciting. I think they'll be good for him. I'm just a little uncomfortable about letting him run about." She arranged a stack of invoices, glancing at them and automatically putting them in some sort of order as she spoke. "Is it safe for them to hunt snakes?"

Jonas chuckled at the worry wrinkles between her brows. "He's a boy. It'll do 'im good."

"Aren't there rattlesnakes?"

"Not as common in these parts as garter or bull snakes. They like the sun, so they mostly stay out in the open. They're sit-and-wait predators and avoid people. You get a warning with the tail, too."

Her eyes widened, and he didn't know if he was helping or hurting by trying to explain. "If you see one," he went on, "you leave it be and it leaves you alone. People don't get bit unless they bother 'em or try to pick 'em up. Matt and Danny know that. They'll teach Tyler."

She gave him a speculative look. "How do you know all this?"

"I was a boy once."

"How do boys learn such things?"

He stacked a couple of ledgers and pushed the pen and ink toward her. "Same way girls learn to have tea parties. Instinct, I reckon."

She gathered as much as she could carry, and Jonas asked Quay to help him load a few crates and then carry them down the street.

He called upon Ward to rearrange the room behind the hotel clerk's area, directing the moving of cartons and chairs to unearth an old desk. Originally intended for an office, the room was away from the traffic of the foyer and the dining room, but it had become a depository for lost items.

He was certain Eliza Jane was accustomed to far more lavish surroundings. "I'll have the place cleaned up tomorrow," he told her.

"I'm the cleaning help, remember?" she said with a smile.

"Not for a week or two, you're not. You're my right hand."

She directed her gaze to his hand where it extended from the sling. Her eyes seemed unnaturally shiny. Was she going to cry?

Ward entered and set down another crate of files. "Here, boss?"

"That's good. Thanks."

Eliza Jane removed her bonnet and stood to the side, waiting until Ward left.

"Somethin' I said?" Jonas asked.

She shook her head, but didn't meet his eyes.

"Doesn't improve my day to make ladies cry," he said.

She set the pen and ink she'd been holding on the desktop. "Jenny once told me I was her right hand. Not literally, of course, not like you meant it, but because she couldn't manage without me."

He didn't know what to say. She'd been such a tower of strength whenever he'd spoken with her. Her grief was a hard thing to see. "If you need some time…before startin' to work on this…before workin' at all…"

"No, I don't. I need to work."

To keep busy? Then why would her brother-in-law disapprove? Jonas had picked up on her desperation more than once. Her insistence indicated she truly needed the money, though he couldn't understand why. Intuitively he suspected there was more to her and her situation than met the eye. More than she was letting on.

After watching her from this side of the street while she made her way to the tearoom those many afternoons, it seemed like fortuity that she was right here.

A black tendril of her hair had come loose and hung alongside her face. He noticed the winged shape of her eyebrow and the delicate curve of her cheek with a cautionary warning in his gut. She was too vulnerable, too naive to know his undisciplined thoughts when he looked at the slope of her breasts beneath her white shirtwaist or let his attention waver to the curve of her lips.

What was it about this woman that unsettled him? Admittedly, he had a weakness where females were concerned, but it was a protective instinct, a fighting urge that had been born one night twenty-five years ago, the night he'd been helpless to protect the woman who'd needed him.

This was different. He felt protective toward Eliza Jane, yes, but more…he was drawn to her by a compelling fascination…and yet wary, like a moth fluttering near a flame.

"Today's a bust," he said, deciding. "Tomorrow'll be soon enough to get the payroll done."

Her amber eyes were wide, showing her confusion when she looked at him. Such an unusual combination, that hair and those eyes. Had it only been the night before that he'd kissed her?

He shouldn't have done that.

He wanted to kiss her again.

He wanted to satisfy this bone-deep quest to somehow *reach* her. The craving was the confoundedest thing he'd ever felt.

Stepping to a shelf beside the door, he reached for

two keys lying in the dust. He extended one. "If you can't sleep tonight and you want, come on down and clean the place to your likin'."

She reached for the key, careful not to let her fingers brush his, and nodded. As though she'd picked up on his foolhardy thoughts, she backed away and hurried out the door.

That night, he used his better judgment, took the doc's medicine early on and slept like a rock.

A startled shriek woke him.

Jonas rolled to his good side and squinted at Francine Kluver. "What?"

"I didn't know you were still sleeping! You've never been here before when I came to make the bed! I'm so sorry, Mr. Black. I shoulda knowed when I saw your water pitcher still sittin' outside the door." The housekeeper had turned around and was talking over her shoulder.

He reached for the sheet and dragged it to cover his lower half. The movement shot pain through his right side. He stifled a groan to sit on the edge of the bed. "What time is it?"

"Eight-thirty or thereabouts," she replied.

"Will you get me that water and then a cup of coffee, please?"

"Want me to reheat it?"

He shook his head, and then realized she wasn't looking at him. "No."

"Right away." She shot out the door and returned with the pitcher, her face turned away. "Here ya go."

She set the pitcher on his bureau and fled, the outer door slamming behind her.

Jonas poured the tepid water into the ironstone bowl, dipped a cloth, washed and dried. Everything took longer using his left hand. He finally worked up lather in his shaving cup and dabbed it on his face.

Awkwardly, he picked up the razor, got it open and made a first attempt to scrape it over his beard, nicking himself with the first stroke. He hissed as a knock sounded at the door.

"C'mon in," he called. "Set it out there, I'll come get it."

"Come get what?" Eliza headed toward the sound of Jonas's voice. She'd cleaned last night, and started on the ledgers early this morning. There were a few things she needed to clarify before she finalized the numbers.

Entering his room, she stopped in her tracks. Jonas stood in front of the massive bureau. The first thing she noticed was the length of his legs, followed by the arresting shape of his bare backside and the width of his broad shoulders. Her heart chugged to a halt at the same time her feet stopped moving.

An oak frame suspended the mirror in which she saw his lathered face, dark eyes staring back at her, and the image of a rock-solid chest. Her heart started up again, but at a breakneck speed.

"What is this, the Union Pacific station this morning?" he asked.

"You said to come in!"

"I thought you were Francine!" He swished the razor in a bowl of water and shook his head.

The red-haired housekeeper was welcome to walk into his bedroom while he was buck naked?

"Not like that!" he added. "I mean I thought you'd stop out there!"

"You said come in!" she repeated.

They'd been shouting at each other since she'd spotted him and he'd recognized her.

"She's bringing coffee," he explained.

Eliza turned on her heel and shot into the sitting room, the image of his sleekly muscled body foremost in her mind. The picture would be lodged there for the rest of her life.

"Eliza Jane?" he called.

"I'm going down to the office."

"I'll be there shortly."

"Take your time." She fled into the hall and leaned against the wall, her hand pressed to her breast, her face hot.

Francine approached carrying a tray holding a cup of coffee and a covered plate. They looked at each other. Did Jonas have something going on with this young woman?

"Did you just walk in there?" Francine asked with wide-eyed concern.

Eliza's head felt light. She nodded.

"Was Mr. Black out of bed?"

Mr. Black? "He certainly was."

"Is he mad?"

"I think so."

Francine nodded. "Want to take this tray in?"

Eliza shook her head.

"Will you stand right there while I do?"

"Okay."

Francine balanced the tray and knocked. She opened the door and called in, "I've got your tray, Mr. Black! I'm bringing it in now."

The wariness in her voice amused Eliza, and the humor in the situation struck her. "Did you walk in there earlier?"

Francine looked back. "I thought he was gone and I went to make his bed. He was still lyin' in it." She called into the room, "I'm setting your tray on the table out here. Your coffee's nice and hot."

"Thanks," he returned. "Let's forget this mornin', can we?"

"Yes, sir, Mr. Black. Done forgot it already."

She hurried back to the hall, pulling the door closed behind her. She looked at Eliza, and Eliza saw the worry drain from her face. Francine pursed her lips as though holding back a smile.

Laughter welled up in Eliza at the same time. They both turned and ran for the stairway before humor got the best of them. They held it in all the way down the stairs, round the bend in the landing, but their laughter burst out by the time they reached the kitchen.

Eliza laughed until tears ran down her cheeks, and she held her aching side. The release felt wonderful. She hadn't laughed so hard in a good many years, and felt a trifle guilty that it was at Jonas's expense that she did so now.

"What's so all-fired hilarious?" Lilibelle asked from where she stood, stirring something in a kettle on the stove. "I could use a little humor."

Francine straightened, wiped her eyes on her apron and composed herself, but a grin remained on her face as she cleaned up the table where she'd apparently made Jonas's breakfast.

Eliza didn't answer Lilibelle, either, instead taking a deep breath. With a new spring in her step, she headed for the foyer and the clean office where her paperwork waited.

Chapter Eight

Jonas showed up half an hour later, freshly shaven, red nicks dotting his jaw. She'd been waiting for him with her stomach aquiver. How could she look him in the eye and not die of mortification? How would she *ever* look at him and not imagine him just the way she'd seen him? How would she ever stop thinking about Jonas wearing nothing but shaving lather?

"You cut yourself," were the first words out of her mouth.

"I shaved left-handed."

"I could have…" She started to say *helped you,* but then realized the folly of that thought on top of the embarrassing incident.

"What do you say we discuss the mornin' and then put it behind us, so that every time we look at each other, you don't blush and look away?"

She placed the pen in its marble holder, folded her

hands one atop the other and looked him square in the eye. "What is there to say?"

Now that she'd given him her full attention, he flattened his lips in a line and then pursed them, the expression making her suspect he wasn't so sure he knew how to address this particular situation. The cuts he'd dotted with alum still stung, but nothing like the pain that throbbed in his arm and shoulder.

"Do you want an apology?" she asked.

"No." He looked aside briefly and then at her. "*I'm* sorry for your discomfort."

"It's no one's fault," she assured him. "I didn't have the vapors, I won't be having nightmares, and I won't ignore you. I'm quite all right."

"You are?"

"I am."

He gave a satisfied nod. "Good."

"It's a good thing you practiced your apology on me, however, since you'll be presenting it again."

He picked up on her reference. "I need to apologize to Francine, too?"

"I'm thinking of starting a ladies' society," she answered. "Women who've seen Jonas Black naked. There are two of us already. If we ask around, I'm sure we can recruit more."

His dark eyes widened momentarily, and then he laughed. "That was a shockin' thing for a respectable lady to say," he told her, but he was still chuckling.

She couldn't resist laughing herself. His surprise at her unexpected arrival was funny, after all. "Well, it made you laugh, and you were taking yourself far too seriously. Can we get on with the payroll figures now?"

And that easily, the morning's incident was relegated to a matter they had laughed about.

As they worked, Jonas listened to her suggestions and asked her opinion more than once. It was impossible not to compare his easy acceptance and respect for her ideas to her father's bullheaded certainty that she wasn't capable of anything more than following directions.

When they broke for lunch, he invited her to join him in the dining room. She asked him a question about a particular delivery that had been a problem a few days earlier.

"That's work, and this is lunch." His smile was a little strained, and she guessed his arm was bothering him.

Ward appeared at the doorway, Luther Vernon beside him. Ward spotted them at their table and pointed. Luther headed for them. He was a big man, and the black suit he wore with a white shirt had to have been custom-made for his frame.

"Someone's here," she alerted Jonas as he approached.

Looking up, Jonas set down his fork. "Afternoon, Mr. Vernon."

Luther held his hat in one hand, a folded piece of paper in the other. "Black."

"Got somethin' for me?"

He held out the paper. "I have a message for Miss Sutherland."

Eliza wiped her fingers on her napkin and took it from him.

"I'll wait for your answer."

Eliza turned the paper over, recognizing the parchment and the seal as the same her father had always used. The sight made her miss him at the same time it jabbed a splinter of fear into her heart. Royce had taken over everything in her life that had once been good, and he had twisted it into something despised. She slid her fingers beneath the fold, broke the wax and opened the missive.

I'll be joining you in the dining hall for supper at seven sharp. See that Tyler is in bed for the night. I won't have his schedule disrupted.

At Royce's demand, resentment rose up strong. He'd probably written this from the comfort of her father's chair, even using the man's pen while posing as someone important. A real man had to earn respect, and Royce didn't have it in him to earn anything more than disgust. He controlled people, rather than led them. Fear tempered Eliza's indignation and she took a calming breath.

She glanced up at Jonas, who seemed curious, but who had politely looked down to study his plate. Luther stood waiting.

Royce knew she wouldn't refuse. He was still controlling her, even though she'd moved from the house. She couldn't defy him. The secret he wielded like a loaded gun had the power to destroy her life. He'd become a man of influence in this town, the man holding the Sutherland purse strings. He reveled in the power it gave him. "Tell him I'll be waiting at seven."

Luther turned and headed for the door.

Eliza placed the note in her pocket. "My brother-in-law will be joining me for supper."

"He probably misses his boy."

She said nothing, but noticed Jonas had only picked at the steaming chicken and noodles on his plate. Eliza reached over and placed the backs of her fingers against his cheek.

Jonas glanced up in surprise.

"You're warm," she told him. "You should be resting."

"I do feel a mite tuckered, that's for sure," he replied.

"Why don't you go lie down after lunch? Lock the door," she added.

After a halfhearted smile, he drank from a glass of water and glanced around the room at the serving girls and the customers. "Solid idea."

Eliza finished her meal, and then the two of them left the room, Jonas heading for the stairs.

Her reaction to that note or invitation or whatever it had been was disturbing. Her demeanor had changed the instant she'd seen Vernon. Jonas grew increasingly curious about Eliza Jane every time he observed something like that. She'd been wary around him at first, but he liked the fact that she seemed comfortable now. She even teased and occasionally stood up to him. It bothered him that there were things he didn't know about her. He had no right to pry, but he could sure observe. He planned to keep an eye on her and on all the activities going on around here…but for now he needed to rest.

Eliza asked Ada if Tyler could spend an hour or so with her boys that evening, and the woman was glad to accommodate them. "How far do you live from the hotel?" Eliza asked.

"Our house is behind Doc and Etta's," Ada told her. "It faces east on Birch Street. But Daniel can see he gets home."

"No, I'm sure a walk will do me good after supper." Once she was certain that sending Tyler home with them would be no trouble, Eliza thanked her.

For the rest of the afternoon, whenever Eliza thought of Royce, she felt sick. The hotel dining room was a public place, she assured herself. Her brother-in-law cared about appearances, and he would use this opportunity to make them look like two people sharing their grief.

"He's not worth the nickel it would cost to put a bullet in his head," she said aloud, shocking herself with her train of thought and her fierce animosity. For Tyler's sake, she had to control her feelings.

She was still telling herself that a few hours later, as she stood brushing out her hair while Tyler sat at the desk. He finished adding the numbers on his slate and turned it so she could see the sum.

"You're such a bright and clever fellow," she told him, walking over to cradle his chin and rub her thumb against his freckled cheekbone.

"Mama always said that," he told her. He laid down the slate and chalk and stared at the desktop. "I miss Mama. An' I miss my room."

Eliza knelt where he sat and urged him to turn and face her. She placed her hands on his knees and looked into his blue eyes, now swimming with tears. "I know you do, sweetie. I miss her, too."

A tear rolled down his cheek and sliced another shred from her already-ragged heart. "You won't get sick, will you, Aunt Liza?"

His fear of losing her made her all the more determined to see that he didn't. "You don't have to worry about that. I won't get sick, and I won't leave you. Not ever."

He leaned forward and wrapped his arms around her neck as he had so often when he was younger, trapping her hair in the hug, but she didn't care. She didn't take his trust lightly. She would do everything in her power to see that he had a good life.

A tap sounded at the door. Eliza kissed his cheek and stood. "That's probably Daniel. You mind your manners at Mrs. Harper's, and I'll come for you later."

"Yes'm."

After Daniel and Tyler had gone, she finished her hair, pinning it up and completing her ensemble with her timepiece and a lace collar Jenny Lee had crocheted.

She took a seat at the south corner of the dining room, well away from the kitchen where the other hotel employees normally sat. From her location she could see the foyer and noticed Ward greet several dinner guests.

Royce appeared promptly at seven. She observed as he gave his bowler to Ward, who placed it under the counter. Her brother-in-law spotted her and made his way to the table.

"Good evening, my dear." His polite tone belied the repulsive way his eyes raked over her. He aligned the silverware to his satisfaction and placed the napkin in his lap.

She didn't respond audibly to the greeting or the glower, but her skin crawled.

He picked up the menu and looked it over. The hotel purchased fresh meat and vegetables, and Lilibelle planned menus with adequate choices. The portions were generous and the meals tasty. She wondered what he would find to criticize.

He scanned the list of dishes. "Black needs to put a gun to the customers' heads to charge these prices."

She looked away. She'd already seen the fare and knew what she was having.

Her wandering gaze caught upon Jonas entering the dining room with Silas Bowers who ran Silver Bend's local paper, the *Big Sky Sentinel*. The two men seated themselves at a table about three away from where Eliza sat, and both men glanced over at the same time.

Polite greetings were exchanged, with her brother-in-law even getting up to greet Silas with a handshake. Jonas offered Royce his right hand by raising the arm with the sling. Royce gave it a firm shake. Watching, Eliza winced, but Jonas held a polite smile.

Royce wouldn't be visibly rude in front of Silas or where anyone could witness. He was vigilant in making a good impression. He sat back down and placed his hand over Eliza's in what was meant to look like a reassuring gesture, but one that she recognized as possessive. She wanted to jerk away, but forced herself to be still.

"You earned my displeasure with the Vernet, Eliza Jane. That was a stupid thing to do."

"It was the least I could do for Nora."

"You had to have known you would pay."

Nadine worked her way through the tables to theirs. "How are you, this evening? What can I get for you?"

"Fine, thanks," Eliza replied. "I'd like the rainbow trout with rice, please. And tea."

Royce ordered roast beef.

Nadine moved to take orders at another table.

The banker, Ed Phillips, and his wife took a table nearby. Royce greeted him like an old friend, and they chatted for a moment.

Royce turned his attention back to Eliza. "I'm removing thirty days from your reprieve," he said in a low voice.

"What do you mean?" she asked warily.

"I've moved up our wedding date. You now have two months to prepare yourself. We'll make the announcement at the end of June and be married the end of July."

Taken aback by his announcement, she forced herself to keep her voice level. "That's scandalous! My sister's only been gone a few days."

"She's been out of the picture far longer than that.

She was on her deathbed for an eternity, dragging out that whole messy ordeal, but she was missing from the public. Most of them hadn't seen her for months."

At his callous cruelty, anger roared through Eliza's veins. Heat stung her neck and face. She wanted to pick up something big and heavy and wallop him. "If there was any justice in this world, you would be struck by lightning right this very moment."

Royce smiled. "That fire is seductive, as you well know. I can hardly keep my hands to myself when you talk that way."

Eliza thought she was going to faint. Discreetly, she dipped the corner of her napkin in the glass of cold water sitting before her and dabbed the moisture against her temples and at the base of her throat. She could still carry out her plan. She had perhaps six paydays with which to make do before she had to cut and run. Six weeks to deal with this man and pretend that she was succumbing to his blackmail. She could do it.

"You're concerned about what people think," she said, "but they'll think you're disloyal to Jenny if you announce you're marrying me so soon."

"Nonsense. They'll understand a man's need to take a wife, and respect that I care enough about my family to keep it intact."

The images that flashed through her mind made her want to run screaming from the dining room. But she couldn't. She had to take care of Tyler. Eliza sneaked a glance at Jonas and found him observing them. She managed a weak smile.

Royce noted their interaction and reached for her hand once again. "You'll be sorry if you cross me. And your loose morals are unattractive. Stay clear of that man. He wouldn't want you if he knew everything I do about you. You're fortunate I want you. But then my cravings are a trifle more...*unconventional*."

Nadine brought a tray with their food, and Eliza withdrew, wiping her hand on her napkin in her lap, wishing she had soap and water.

The trout was delicious, but her stomach was in such a state, she barely picked at her meal. Royce, on the other hand, ate his with gusto. When he finished, he dabbed at his pencil-thin mustache with the napkin, then drank his coffee.

Upon Nadine's return, Royce instructed her to place their meals on Sutherland's tab. "And add the Phillips's dinners, as well. Your meals are on me," he called over to Ed.

The couple thanked him profusely.

Of course he buttered up the banker. The fact that Royce was using Sutherland money however he pleased rankled Eliza. He had to keep the man safely in his pocket for the future.

"Good business," he said to Eliza.

She looked away. Tacky business. Nowhere near the same class as her father.

"Is that all you're eatin'?" Nadine asked her.

"It was delicious, I'm just not very hungry," she replied.

"My dear sister-in-law is suffering," Royce told the other woman. "Grief, is so disabling, you know. It pains me to see Eliza Jane like this. That's why I want to be here for her whenever I can."

Nadine nodded and took away their plates.

"Are you ready to leave?" Royce asked, standing.

"I believe I'll stay and enjoy another cup of tea," she told him loud enough for the nearby couple to hear. "Tea comforts me in my grief."

Though his eyes held enmity, he bowed politely. "Very well, my dear. Have a good night, and send for me should you need anything at all."

He spoke to Ed again and then left the room.

Nadine had brought her a ceramic pot, so she poured a fresh cup of tea and added a cube of sugar. Once she knew Royce was well on his way, she stood to go.

Jonas and Silas had finished their supper and stood in the foyer, deep in conversation.

Eliza used her key to let herself into the office and grab the shawl she'd left across the back of a chair.

Jonas spotted Eliza Jane heading for the door. Her stilted demeanor over dinner had him puzzled. Some of the looks she'd given Royce had to have singed his hair. "Goin' out?" he asked.

Silas had headed out a moment before.

"I'm going to gather up Tyler at Ada's," she replied.

"Wait for me. I need to stop by Doc's and it's right on the way." He leaned behind the front desk to grab his hat and settled it on his head.

The cool night air felt good on Jonas's face, but Eliza pulled her shawl up over her head.

He had noticed the undeniable change that came over

her when Royce Dunlap was around. She seemed…
irritated when she looked at him or spoke to him. Resentful even, but that didn't match what Jonas knew of
her character. And that baffling here-and-gone glimmer
of panic in her eyes whenever her brother-in-law was
mentioned disturbed him.

"Everything all right?" he asked.

"Yes, of course."

They were headed east on Main Street, passing first
the square window at the *Big Sky Sentinel* where everything inside was dark. And then a few feet later the
batwing doors of the Silver Star where light spilled out
onto the boardwalk and music jangled from a piano. He
recognized Curly Jack's lively rendition of "Golden
Slippers."

They crossed the street and Jonas pointed down the
adjacent block. "I want to stop at Doc's for a minute."

She joined him, walking alongside him toward the
small square house.

Jonas paused at the curb, fighting back the disturbing images that assailed him every time he set foot on
this property. He'd gone in there the night he'd been
shot. He'd seen for himself that the place had changed
over the years. But seeing it still hadn't erased the
memories or the trauma.

Whenever he saw the house, whenever he thought of
his childhood, he thought of that night.

Chapter Nine

"Something wrong?" she asked.

Jonas tried to shake off the memories. "Takes me a minute," he answered, then stepped up to the brick sidewalk.

"What takes a minute?"

"To remember who I am."

"What are you talking about?"

He looked down at her. She'd lived here all her life. He figured she'd heard the stories. "You don't know what happened in this house?"

She shook her head.

He glanced from her to the light glowing behind the yellow-and-white checkered curtains. He saw the rooms as they'd been back then. Remembered his mother's sewing basket and the picture of a sailing ship that had hung on the wall above the heating stove.

"When I was growin' up my father was a cavalry doctor. Gone treatin' soldiers for months at a stretch."

He paused, caught up in the past. "My mother took care of the house and did all the normal things like cookin' and laundry. I helped with chores. She raised me pretty much by herself. Did a fine job of it, too."

"Obviously."

Her comment distracted him briefly, but he returned to his subject. "Used to read of an evenin'. Sometimes I read to her while she sewed. One night a bunch of outlaws, no older than some of the boys in this town, now that I look back, they got themselves shot up in a gunfight. Came here 'cause someone told 'em it was the doc's house.

"My mother told 'em there was no doctor, that my father was gone. Most likely they were drunk."

Jonas remembered his fear vividly. Remembered feeling helpless. "One of 'em told her to fix his friend's wound or he'd put a bullet in her head."

He turned to find Eliza Jane watching him, listening in earnest for his next words.

In his head, he'd relived that night a million times. He'd dreamed the images over and over again, exactly as they'd happened. But he'd never told anyone. Old-timers in Silver Bend, the people he mingled with, already knew the story. He did find it interesting that the incident was so well forgotten in the community that she'd never heard it.

"I saw the whole thing happen," he told her. "Watched it all. They just laughed and jostled me back and forth between 'em like a rag doll. Wasn't anything I could do."

"It hurts me just to hear this," she said, and her voice was a little shaky. "How old were you?"

"Ten."

"Only a couple years older than Tyler."

Jonas had never looked at a young boy and compared his own age at the time, but now that he did, he understood exactly why he'd been defenseless. He nodded. "My mother begged them to leave, but they wouldn't stop shoutin' and threatening her. It was when one of 'em held the gun to *my* head that she ended up doing the best she could."

There had been so much blood. His mother's hands and her dress had been saturated with it.

"Fella died right there on the floor. Then the one holdin' me let me go…and shot her."

He'd run to where she lay, the blood seeping from her chest only adding to the crimson patches already soaking her clothing.

Jonas stopped breathing for a moment, his eyes closed against the suffering.

"I'm so sorry, Jonas," Eliza Jane said softly from beside him.

It had taken only a few brief sentences to explain the horror that had changed his life—and his father's—and shaped him into the man he was today. Glad to have told her, he opened his eyes and found her expression sympathetic in the darkness.

"It was a long time ago," he said, as though that made the telling easier, but time hadn't healed all the wounds; that was apparent since he couldn't come here without feeling sick. "I stayed with a family till my father got word and came home. She'd been buried by then. After that…well, that's what started him drinkin'. That and all he'd seen on the battlefields."

"I never knew," she said.

"I stuck around a couple years, but I lit out when I was thirteen."

"You told me about your years after that. But eventually you came back."

"Couldn't let 'im die alone. He loved her. Never had a moment's peace after she died. Blamed himself."

"As did you."

He looked down at her. "No. I blamed him, too. I was just a kid. As helpless as she was. Shoulda been someone takin' care of us."

"Everyone needs someone to take care of them," she agreed.

They still stood on the brick path. Jonas gestured toward the house. "Doc told me t' come by and have my arm looked at. Hope he doesn't mind the hour."

He took her elbow as they walked forward and stepped onto the small wooden platform that served as a porch. Jonas rapped on the door.

Etta opened it. "Come in, the two of you. Jonas, are you all right?"

He swept off his hat. "Yes'm."

Etta kept Eliza company in the small comfortable sitting room while Jonas disappeared through a door with the doctor. A short while later, Jonas returned with his arm freshly bandaged and in a clean sling.

"He needs to rest," Dr. McKee told her. "The wound's a little red and he still has a fever."

They crossed to Ada's house by walking through the dark yards instead of going back to the street and around, and this way came up behind the place.

Each time Jonas shared something about himself, she felt a little closer to him, more at ease in his company. Being around him every day, and interacting with the others at the hotel, was bringing her back to a place where she didn't feel as isolated as she had for so long.

Eventually, Eliza had Tyler's hand snugly in hers and they started back. From three blocks away, the piano could be heard, but out here darkness enveloped them.

"Kinda scary at night, ain't it?" Tyler asked.

"I like it," Jonas replied. "Slept on the ground under the sky plenty of nights when I was a soldier. When it's clear, you can see all the stars and even find the Big Dipper."

"We read about The Big Dipper in school. It looks like a big ladle. Where is it?"

Jonas took his hat off so he could lean his head back and survey the sky. "The easiest to find. There," he said, kneeling beside Tyler and pointing. "Points to other stars if you know how to look. By locatin' it, you can always find your direction."

Eliza was more fascinated by watching the two of them than by the heavens.

"I heard tell that in Africa, they see the Big Dipper as a drinkin' gourd," Jonas told the boy. "Runaway slaves from the south used to follow the drinkin' gourd to the north and their freedom."

"Did you learn that at school? Miss Fletcher never told us that part."

"Learned it from a free slave," he answered.

"You know free slaves?"

"Yup. Know some Indians, too. Cherokee scout told me the handle part is three cubs followin' their mama." Jonas stood and Tyler stayed close at his side.

"The Iroquois say," he continued, "that one spring a long time ago a great bear wandered far and wide throughout the sky. He hunted and fished until he was full and happy. But then one day three young braves ran after him to kill him so they'd have his fur for a warm blanket and food for their families. The bear ran and ran from them all summer long. The braves outsmarted him and caught up. They pierced him with their arrows and he died. The bear's blood poured out all over the sky and even made the leaves turn red and orange. Then the trees dropped their leaves in mourning."

"I saw leaves turn red and orange," Tyler said.

"The story doesn't end there," Jonas assured him. "The great bear was reborn in the spring, and the braves set out after him again. Now they do this every year. So if you look into the sky you can see the braves trailin' behind the great bear."

For several minutes Tyler seemed absorbed with finding the bear and hunters. At last they moved on. "Where did you go in the army?" Tyler asked as they reached Main Street. "Did you have a black horse?"

"I went lots of places, and I rode a brown horse. He's

livin' out his years in a pasture on Willie Grimshaw's farm."

"Lilibelle's family?" Eliza asked.

"Her pa," Jonas answered.

"Do you visit him?" Tyler asked.

"Yup."

"What's his name?"

"Jeremiah."

"After the Bible? Can I see him?"

"You can see him."

"Oh, boy! When can we go?"

"Tyler, mind your manners," Eliza admonished. "It's not polite to invite yourself."

"That's okay, Tyler," Jonas said. "Sometimes a man needs to speak up for what he wants. How about we ride out when my arm is out of this sling?"

"Yes! Can I, Aunt Liza?"

They reached the hotel, where Jonas opened the door and ushered them into the lobby. Tyler shot up the stairs ahead of them, and the adults followed more slowly. On the second floor, Jonas told her good-night.

"Take your medicine and get a good night's sleep," she said. "And…" She made a motion as if she was turning a key.

"Don't worry," he replied, heading for his quarters.

Between thoughts of Eliza and the old memories that had risen to the surface, his head was spinning. Add to that the fever and, although he hated the drugging effects of the pain medicine, Jonas had to admit he needed it that night.

He slept hard and woke sweating several times. Each time he wiped his skin with cool water. The last time it was still dark, but he couldn't go back to sleep.

He lit the lamps and went downstairs for fresh water and a slice of pie. Using one arm, it took two trips, but eventually he ate the dessert and drank thirstily.

He'd slept that afternoon, so he knew that was why he was having trouble now. As he paced his sitting room, the trunk that had been placed against the wall caught his attention. Ward and Pool had carried it up the day before. It had been among his father's belongings, and he'd moved it from place to place, finally leaving it in the storeroom until they'd needed that space for an office.

The latch held a padlock that had never worked, but there was nothing of value inside. Opening the lid, Jonas knelt to view the contents.

There was a blue-and-white ceramic humidor filled with odds and ends of tie tacks, coins and two pocket watches. Lifting a folded coat, he found two packets of letters tied with string. Untying them, he discovered dozens of letters from his parents to each other.

Jonas opened one and read it quickly. His father spoke of the weather, briefly of skirmishes and the locations, and penned words of his love for his wife and how much he missed her. A quick glance showed all of the missives similar. Jonas didn't want to read those particular words. He wasn't prepared to change his thinking of the man as he'd believed him to be all these years, so he retied the bundles and buried them between a few books.

A stack of ledgers caught his attention, and he pulled one out with his good hand and used the fingers of his opposite to open it. Rather than accounts or numbers on the pages of the leather-bound book, he discovered line after line of the same neat penmanship he'd seen in his father's letters.

Each page was dated, indicating a year Jonas had been away. One entry began with notes on the Kopeke family's bout with a fever and sickness, but after recording his visit to the house, Jonas's father had detailed an amusing incident outside the saloon.

Flipping a few pages, Jenny Lee Sutherland's name caught his eye. Jonas carried the journal to his chair, settled comfortably and began to read.

She's just a slip of a girl. Pale and delicate, but with a zest for life and a powerful love for her family. It saddens me each time I'm called to the house and it pains me not to have a better prognosis for her parents. They've taken her to the best doctors in the East and heard the same from each of them. The girl has a defective heart.

His father's comments were more than clinical remarks; they were an outlet for the events he witnessed and the feelings he had experienced.

Jonas flipped through the pages, locating numerous visits to the Sutherland home as well as the other families of Silver Bend. The reports were as much about the people of the town as they were about their illnesses. Going back to the beginning, he read into the night, learning which families lost babies, which men had been on the town council and occasionally what the sermon had been about on a particular Sunday. The Silver Bend of years ago came alive on the pages of his father's journal.

Jonas woke to sunlight streaking through the split where the drapes came together. His father's journal lay on the floor where it had fallen. He winced as he stood, not only from the pain in his shoulder, but from the stiffness in his legs and hips. After stretching, he limped to the window that looked over the street and pulled back the curtain.

Midmorning, the street bustled with horses and wagons. The chalkboard on the walk in front of the bakery read, Cinnamon Buns Warm From the Oven. His stomach growled.

A pitcher of water sat outside his door. He carried it to the bowl in his bedroom, spilling some as he poured.

As he went about his duties that day and the next, he kept thinking of his father's detailed accounts of the community. He put the journals in chronological order and continued reading the accounts, which stemmed from about two years after Jonas had left. Jonas pictured his father alone at night, sitting in the house where his wife had been murdered, a glass of whiskey at his elbow as he recorded the passing of days and events.

Jonas didn't want to, but he was forced to see his

father in a new light. Through the doctor's unfamiliar and revealing viewpoint, his compassion and loneliness were clearly defined.

One afternoon Jonas sat in the office, his thoughts drifting to events about which he'd been reading. Whenever Eliza Jane spoke of his father, it seemed as though she'd known him better than Jonas did, and she probably had. But she'd only known him *afterward,* only seen one side of him.

Eliza Jane held out a stack of receipts and asked a question.

He hadn't been paying attention, so he had to ask her to repeat.

She'd been doing a proficient job of keeping the records for the hotel and saloon, and he'd had to ask for her help in writing out the employment vouchers, as well. She caught on to everything immediately. She must have been a big help to her father. It was pretty clear that her father hadn't appreciated her. Why was it people didn't see what was right in front of them?

"Hold on to those," he told her.

She nodded, but kept her attention on his face.

She was seated at the desk and he at a small table they'd pushed against the back so that they faced each other. "I want to ask you about something not related to the job."

He put down the paper he'd been holding and gave her his attention.

"It will be Tyler's birthday in a few days. Normally, I would ask several of his friends to the house and have a little celebration." She rubbed at a smudge of ink on her index finger. "Since we're staying here, I was wondering if I could ask his friends to come after school and if we might hold our party in the dining room."

"Of course. That's not a busy time of day."

"That's why I thought it would be better than a Saturday. I'll pay for the ingredients and make the cake."

"No need. Lily has barrels of flour and sugar and we've got a couple dozen hens out back."

"But I want to bake it myself."

"Whatever pleases you, Eliza Jane."

She gave him a rare hesitant smile, and the sight went right to his gut, conjuring up that unsettling feeling. Being around her every day made it impossible to ignore that out-of-control sensation he couldn't dislodge. He didn't like being out of control...but he admired every last thing about Eliza Jane, from the sound of her voice and the sometimes funny things she said to the way she pressed her palms against her skirt when she was nervous. He liked how she looked at him, just slightly uncertain and yet provocatively challenging.

"What about Royce?"

"What about him?" she asked, her tone somewhat wary.

"Will he attend during the day?"

"He won't remember," she replied.

"Won't remember his son's birthday?"

"I mean..." She glanced at the papers in front of her. "I mean he'll be working. He'll probably acknowledge Tyler's birthday another way."

"Am I invited?" he asked.

A tiny wrinkle formed between her brows, but then smoothed out when she realized what he referred to. "Yes, of course! If you don't mind boisterous children, that is. You'll love my cake."

He was pretty sure he'd love anything she offered him. In that moment, he allowed himself to think ahead, to imagine something more developing between them. He admitted he had a soft spot for taking care of women, but his inclination toward this one went far beyond protectiveness.

He thought about that kiss they'd shared, and the way she made him feel. He considered the way he'd shared his past with her, actually talked about his mother's death for the first time.

Up till now he'd liked his life just fine. The likelihood of a woman sharing it with him had been vague; there hadn't been a woman he cared for enough to seriously consider it.

But maybe it was time. Maybe a future with Eliza Jane was possible.

Chapter Ten

Tyler's party had garnered the attention of everyone who worked in the hotel. Knowing he'd recently lost his mother, the employees went out of their way to offer a little something to the menu or add a gift to the growing stack on the table against the west wall.

Tyler had shown his mortification with a look of chagrin when she'd suggested a few of the classmates he invited be young ladies. She'd thrown up her hands and assured him the guest list was his choice. Eleven boys, including the Harpers, invaded the dining room.

She and Tyler had gone over the games ahead of time, deciding together. They played Hot Boiled Beans first, sending Timmy Hatcher, who was chosen by age, out of the room, and then hiding a silver dollar. The boys all called to Timmy, who was "it" saying, "Hot boiled beans and bacon for supper! Hurry up before it gets cold!"

Timmy returned to the room and searched for the

dollar while all the others called out that Timmy's supper was getting very cold, cold, sometimes hot or very hot, and then eventually burning, depending on how close or far the lad was from the hidden item. It was such a loud clash of childish voices and laughter, that it drew the hotel staff, who tried to watch unobtrusively, but got just as excited as the children.

Jonas showed up and watched with interest. The dark stubble on his face did nothing to lessen his attractiveness. At least he'd stopped torturing his poor skin by shaving left-handed.

"I didn't realize it would be this noisy," she called over the racket as Mikey Kopeke now searched for the dollar and the others directed him with their calls of temperature.

"They're boys," he said with a shrug. "They should have fun."

After a couple more had searched for the dollar, and Eliza proposed a word game, Jonas took a brass bell from inside his sling and rang it to get their attention. "Have you heard of the bellman?"

"What's this?"

"Tell us."

The boys came running to where he stood.

"One player gets to be the bellman," he said.

"Me! Me!" they all shouted at once.

He held up the hand with the bell to silence them. "All the others are blindfolded."

He turned to Wade, standing in the doorway, who produced a stack of bright new red bandannas.

"The bellman's gonna carry the bell and walk around. He rings it from time to time, and everyone else has to try to catch him."

Hoots of laughter went up as the boys caught on to the game.

"Miss Sutherland will be our first bellman," Jonas added.

"Oh no." She held up a hand.

"Come on, they'll all be blindfolded and you'll be able t' *see* 'em. How hard can it be?"

"I don't think so," she protested.

"C'mon, Aunt Liza," Tyler begged. "*Please* be the bellman."

At his pleading she acquiesced, and then half-a-dozen adults showed up to move tables and chairs against the walls and help blindfold the boys.

"If I'm playing, you're playing," she told Jonas.

"I'm wounded," he reminded her.

"You play that hand *now,* but the rest of the time you manage just fine." She cocked her head. "Are you afraid the boys will be better at it than you?"

He turned and motioned for Ward to bring him a bandanna. "I accept that challenge. And I just made a new rule."

"What's that?"

"The first one to catch you gets the biggest piece of cake."

The boys loved that idea.

"I need help with this," he said, holding the bandanna aloft.

"I'll do it!" Tyler shot forward to take the red fabric from his hand and fold it into a blindfold. "Get lower so I can reach you."

Watching Jonas hunker down so Tyler could help him by wrapping the bandanna around his eyes, Eliza got a catch in her throat. She'd noticed the interaction between them the night they'd studied the Big Dipper and recognized Tyler's admiration when Jonas talked about the army and his horse. Tyler was hungry for a man's attention.

This was how his life should have been.

She caught her wayward thinking and got back to the game. "Back away in a circle," she called out. "Face away from me."

Once the males did as she asked, Eliza stepped to the middle of the room and rang the bell once. They all turned and headed different directions, only one or two actually heading toward her.

She rang it again, and they turned toward her. Silently she moved around to the opposite side of the room and rang it again.

As they turned, and she had to move yet again, Eliza wanted to laugh. She had to hold a hand over her mouth to keep from giving away her position as Danny moved within three feet of her.

She dodged away and rang the bell.

After several similar misses, she stood between Matt Harper and Jonas. Planning to trick them yet again by slipping behind them, she tiptoed behind Jonas.

He spun so quickly she almost tripped in her attempt

to get away, but unerringly, he grabbed her around the waist with his good arm, pulling her back against him.

She didn't fight, because she didn't want to hurt him, but she could feel the hard plane of his chest as he held her fast.

"I got her!" he called.

The boys tore off their blindfolds and Jonas loosened his hold.

"How did you know I was there?" she asked softly.

Without releasing her, he answered, "I could smell your hair."

She pulled away and met his eyes, lit with a teasing yet desirous fire. She backed away, heart pounding. "Who will be the bellman this time?"

"That would be me," he replied good-naturedly, giving her his blindfold and taking the bell from her. "Winner trades places. And don't forget my cake."

"I need to see to the food." She forced herself to walk, not run, toward the kitchen.

Seated on a chair near the kitchen door, Lilibelle, who'd been watching, gave Eliza a smile. "It's good to see you having fun."

Phoebe and Yvonne grinned as she passed.

Eliza stood alone in the kitchen, gathering her wits. That incident had been entirely innocent, played out in front of a dozen children and numerous adults, yet she felt as though their exchange had been intimate.

He'd smelled her hair? She raised her hand to her hair, and found her fingers trembling. It had been the way he'd said it, the way his eyes had smoldered, the way his body felt pressed to hers. She brought a loose tress to her nose. What did she smell like, vanilla? Frosting?

A shout and laughter rose from the other room, reminding her she'd come to do a chore, so she uncovered a tray of sandwiches and carried it back to the dining room.

The boys lit into the sandwiches, followed by apple turnovers Lilibelle had contributed, an assortment of cookies Phoebe and Yvonne provided, and finally Eliza's cake.

"I've been savin' myself," Jonas told her, waiting for her to slice his after the boys had gone through the line. "I'll take the biggest piece now."

She cut a wedge that barely fit on the ironstone dessert plate and handed it to him. "It was my mama's recipe," she told him. "Jenny and I always got this cake on our birthdays."

He took a bite and let his eyes close in exaggerated pleasure. "Will you make me one for my birthday?"

"When is it?"

"October."

She would be long gone by then. "I'll give Lilibelle the recipe in case I'm not here."

His frown created a wrinkle between his dark brows. "Where would you be?"

"I won't be at the hotel by then." She wiped her sticky fingers on a wet cloth. "I might be living elsewhere."

"Your house isn't that far away. Or do you mean elsewhere as in *elsewhere?*"

"Maybe. I don't know." She didn't want to meet his eyes again, so she busied herself with the plates and cups the boys were returning. "Tyler will be opening his presents next, and then we can send the children home to their families."

She called for the boys to gather around, and Tyler opened his gifts: slingshots and carved animals, rubber balls, jacks and even a book. He thanked his classmates.

Jonas produced a small brown-paper-wrapped object from his pocket and handed it to Tyler.

Tyler unrolled the paper, revealing a black cylindrical object, trimmed with brass. "This is terrific!"

"What is it?" Eliza asked.

Not sharing her confusion, Tyler proceeded to extend it and peer through one end, showing her that the object was a telescope.

"Just like the army scouts use," Jonas told him.

The boys crowded around, waiting for turns to look through the lenses. Jonas helped her sort the pile of schoolbooks and lunch pails by the door, and eventually all of the children had gone home.

"Thank Jonas for the gift and for letting us have your party here," she told the boy.

Tyler's face was flushed with pleasure and excitement. "This was the best birthday I ever had in my whole life," he told Jonas solemnly.

Jonas had pulled a chair out to rest his arm on a nearby table. "Thanks for invitin' me."

Impulsively, Tyler dashed forward to throw his arms around Jonas's neck.

Jonas's surprised gaze rose to Eliza's. Tears stung her eyes, but she couldn't look away. "Thank you," she wanted to say, but no words would come out.

She hadn't known many men, Eliza realized as she helped return the dining room to order and dried the plates and glasses Nadine had already washed. She'd come in contact with men at the foundry, but never actually gotten to know any. Her father and Forest and Royce were the examples she'd seen. Her father had loved her, but he'd placed little value on her or her abilities.

She'd believed Forest had loved her. It still hurt to know she'd given him her heart and he'd left without so much as an explanation.

And Royce. He did only what was good for Royce, at the expense of others.

Jonas, on the other hand, went out of his way to help people. And there was no price tag on his help. His kindness held a powerful appeal.

After sandwiches and cake and cookies, Tyler couldn't hold much supper, and Eliza wondered how many parents were questioning her wisdom at that hour. She read to him, and he practiced his numbers. Perhaps giving him a bath would settle him down, so she checked the area in the northeast portion of the first level, which was accessible through a hallway behind the parlor, finding the chamber available.

One of the rooms was for guests to use, with the help of the staff to heat water and provide towels, and the other was for employees. Right behind the rooms with the tubs, on the very corner of the building was the laundry facility, with a pump and two stoves for heating water. The whole time she heated and poured Tyler's water, she was planning to return for some relaxing time herself.

Once Tyler was bathed and sound asleep for the night, she read until the hotel was silent. Then Eliza gathered clean clothing and padded down the back stairs.

Again, she stoked the small heater that warmed the bathing room, and then heated water, carrying a pailful from the laundry room to the huge enamel tub.

Jonas had spared no extravagance in the building of these facilities. There were warming racks beside the heater for towels. The tub had a plug that when unstopped, drained out of doors into irrigation pipes that watered the gardens.

She added a splash of her sandalwood cologne and swished it around in the water, thinking about him, about his face when Tyler had hugged him, about the feel of his arms around her waist. Returning for the last of the water on the stove, she nearly ran into the man she'd had on her mind. He held a full pail in his left hand. "Got it."

"Did you bank the stove?" she asked.

He walked past her to dump the steaming water in the tub. "There's one more kettle on. This one may have gotten a little too hot."

"You didn't have to carry it for me."

"I don't mind." He set down the pail.

"I'm not used to people…doing things for me."

"That's a shame." He scratched his jaw with his thumb.

He'd always been cleanly shaven, so not being able to do it properly must be frustrating. She'd ignored the thought the last time she'd had it, but this time she couldn't. She pulled a chair from the corner. "Sit."

"What for?"

"I'm going to shave you."

He raised his eyebrows in uncertainty. "Have you ever done it?"

"Many times. I took care of my father for the better part of a year."

His gaze went to the tub of steaming water. "Right now?"

"We have hot water." She glanced at the open shelves. "Soap and a razor I'm assuming. What more do we need?"

He sat. "Razor and all are stored up there."

"Which basket?" she asked, glancing at the shelves.

"First one on the left. Top shelf," he said, pointing. "There's a cake of Williams."

"Supplies in two places?"

"I spent several years livin' out of saddlebags. I'm enjoying my little luxuries now."

"Nothing wrong with that." She took down the basket, finding his shaving mug and dipping it in her bathwater. "I like how everyone has their own place to leave things as they see fit."

"I like how my employees are trustworthy enough to do that."

"Why wouldn't they be? Most of them you've pulled from one scrape or another." The more she learned of those who worked at the hotel, the more she discovered about Jonas and his proclivity to help people in need. He was kind, yet direct and decisive.

"Some," he said with a shrug.

She dipped a hand towel in the bathwater and wrung it out. She liked his strength and the way he seemed in control of his environment. Each day her respect for him grew. "Tip your head back."

He obeyed and she folded the towel, placing it on his face.

"That feels good," he said, his voice muffled.

She scraped shavings from the cake of soap and stirred it into lather. He was a man with a moral code and a sense of right and wrong to be admired. After removing the towel, she dabbed the shaving suds on his beard.

He watched as she opened the razor and leaned over him. Placing her left hand on his head, she tilted it to the side and drew the blade down his cheek in front of his ear in a smooth stroke, then repeated. When she got to his jaw, he angled his head more, and the razor revealed a scar she hadn't noticed before. "What happened here?"

"What d' you mean?"

"There's a scar."

"Don't recall for sure. I've been in a few fights. Knuckles probably."

The next stroke revealed another white line, this one a little longer and deeper.

Jonas watched her pause and study his jaw. "Remember that one. Thrown from a horse," he told her.

The room was so warm and humid, it became difficult to take a deep breath. The scent of her hair filled his senses, and the touch of her hands set him on fire. Her hair, the color of a shiny raven's wing, hung over her shoulder and across her breast.

He'd noticed her breasts right off. Through the shiny material of her wrapper, every curve was accentuated, and each place drops of water had splashed, her skin stuck to the fabric.

Her eyes, lit with amber fire in the gaslight, met his. Something passed between them, something wordless and *knowing*...something that told him she felt the heat, too, and it wasn't just the warmth of the fire in the heater.

She threaded her fingers into his hair and tipped his head back to shave his neck. His scalp tingled where she touched him.

"Ned never does it that way," he said, suppressing a grin. Ned May was the barber a few doors down.

"I guess you could've gone to Ned's," she told him.

"Not open this late."

Putting her thumb against his nose, she shaved his upper lip in quick smooth motions, one side, then the other. Methodical as with everything else she did. She dotted his chin with more lather and made a couple extra strokes.

"I like your way," he told her, pleased with the tinge of pink that stained her cheeks at his praise.

She rinsed the towel and used it to wipe his face.

Jonas wrapped his fingers around her wrist gently, halting her movement. "Like the way you do every last thing, matter of fact."

Her gaze touched his eyes, his lips. Her pulse was visible in the hollow of her throat, and her skin glowed with moisture. Gently, he took the warm wet towel from her and wiped her forehead, her neck, touched it to her cheek.

"I can't stop thinkin' about you," he admitted. "And that kiss. Have you thought about it?"

Her answer came without hesitation. "Yes."

"Did you like it?"

"Too much," she replied on a ragged breath.

"Enough to do it again?"

"Yes."

"Kiss me now then," he urged.

She placed her damp hand against his cheek and stroked her thumb over his freshly shaven skin. He understood that her hesitation wasn't a lack of willingness, but a ploy to draw out the moment to her satisfaction. He liked that about her, too.

Bending at the waist, her wrapper drooped open, exposing her cleavage framed in delicate ivory lace. His gaze wavered to her breasts. She noticed.

He met her eyes again, held her gaze as she lowered her head and brought her lips to his.

With the warm soft contact, her eyelids fluttered shut. The feel of her mouth on his demanded his full attention, so if it hurt to reach for her with both hands, no pain registered. He returned her kiss of wonder and discovery, wanting more, but needing to savor each moment.

Heart pounding, Eliza withdrew to study his expression, to look into his eyes, to appreciate…

She read desire in his gaze, felt it in the heat of his hands where they held her, one on her shoulder, the other on her back. Wanting to be closer, she turned her body so she could sit on his lap. Touching her cheek to his, she wrapped her arms around his solid shoulders.

He rubbed her back through her satin wrapper, brought a hand to her shoulder and stroked her hair. "You're so soft and warm, Eliza Jane," he said near her ear.

Pleasure tingled across her shoulders and arms at the words and the touch of his breath.

He cupped her jaw and tilted her face so he could look at her in the gaslight. "I had my eye on you when you didn't know I was lookin'," he said. "Days you walked to the tea shop, I was watchin' for you."

His words did crazy things to her heart. Frightened her. Delighted her.

"You're the prettiest woman I ever laid eyes on," he said.

It was easy to be swept away by this man and the flattering manner in which he spoke. Even better was the way he *listened*…as if he really cared about what she had to say…the way he held her in high regard…how he showed appreciation. If she'd ever felt this special or desirable, she couldn't remember.

The way he wanted her made her head spin…her heart sing…her body throb.

She liked the way *he* looked, too. Admired his solid jaw, the breadth of his shoulders. And she'd seen a lot more of him than he'd seen of her. She smiled to herself. "Your mug wouldn't exactly curdle milk," she told him.

He grinned.

And kissed her. Angling his head this time, so he could taste more of her, wrapping his arm snugly around her. He queried her mouth with the tip of his tongue, and she responded to his invitation by parting her lips and participating in the kiss wholeheartedly.

His kiss did crazy things to her heart, and she enjoyed every second of it. She'd never been kissed like this, never *dreamed* of being kissed like this. At last he drew back so both of them could catch their breath. He slid his fingers inside the front of her wrapper and caressed the curve of her breast.

His touch sent a delicious shiver across her heated skin.

Dipping forward, he pressed his lips to her throat, and then kissed her collarbone before untying the sash at her waist.

The room was warm and humid. It felt good and marginally cooler when her robe gaped open. His gaze lowered to her pastel-ribboned chemise. The look in his eyes matched the exhilaration of his reverent touch. He cupped her breast through the damp cotton. She couldn't breathe.

He drew his hand away, and her disappointment was acute. "Don't reckon I've ever wanted anything as much as I want you," he said. "But I don't want to be sorry. I tease you about bein' a respectable lady, but truth is, Eliza Jane, I admire that, and I won't give you reason to be ashamed."

Eliza appreciated his hesitation. He wasn't the kind of man who took advantage of women. But she could never be sorry for wanting this one thing for herself. All she ever did was see to other people's needs and had put herself last for as long as she could remember. "You believe I'm smart, don't you, Jonas?"

"You know I do."

"Then trust me to make this decision. And don't keep me waiting. I've waited long enough."

Chapter Eleven

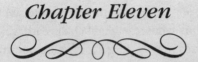

He urged her to her feet and crossed to slide the bolt on the door into place. Reaching with his left arm, he swept every towel from the storage wall to the floor and kicked them into a jumble on the floor.

"Get my buttons," he said, withdrawing his right arm from the sling and pulling the white fabric off over his head with the other arm.

Eliza unbuttoned his shirt and let it fall onto the towels at their feet. The bandage he wore was much smaller than previously, and white gauzy tape wrapped his muscular upper arm.

A jagged scar was evident on his chest, a smaller one on his shoulder.

"What happened here?" she asked, grazing the line with her fingertips.

"Arrow," he replied.

She studied his face. "And this one?"

"Bullet."

"You'd been shot before," she said, surprised.

"Think I wouldn't be such a baby about it, wouldn't ya?"

She laughed, enjoying how he had the ability to make her do that.

He slid her wrapper from one shoulder and then the other, the slick fabric sliding to her feet with a muted swish. "This what respectable ladies are wearin' under their dresses now?" he asked, eyeing her drawers and chemise.

She took pleasure in skimming her palms across the smooth supple skin of his shoulders and then the contrasting texture of his hair-roughened chest. She wanted to press herself into him, become part of him. She sensed that he held himself back for her sake. He was giving her time she didn't want or need.

Without hesitation, so she wouldn't lose her confidence, she loosened the ribbons on her chemise and tugged it off over her head. Her hair caught in it and Jonas reached to untangle the garment, letting it dangle forgotten from his fingers. His gaze caressed her.

Eliza loosened the rest of her underclothing and stepped free of it. He dropped the chemise. As though he sensed what she needed, he guided her to the floor, aligning their bodies, kissing her tenderly at first and then with growing intensity.

Beginning a sensory exploration with his hands and lips, he set her on fire and had her craving more.

Eliza loved the way Jonas made her feel. Because of

the way he valued her, she felt good about herself, felt good about them. Confident. Desirable.

Thinking she might break apart with the sheer pleasure he gave her, she locked her fingers in his hair and opened her mouth against his skin. Tasted him. Breathed him in.

She didn't expect the rush of sensation or the spiraling mixture of delight and astonishment that shimmered through her when he filled her body and told her how perfect she was in every way.

"Did I hurt you?" he asked.

There was no past and no future, only this exhilarating mind-numbing perfect moment. She refused to allow the thought that she was deceiving him spoil one second. "No," she assured him.

It couldn't matter right now that he was her one desperate shot at satisfying her selfish need for acceptance— that he was the one who stood to be hurt. Eliza hadn't anticipated the now-focused pleasure escalating and intensifying until she burst against him.

He kissed her eyelids, met the ragged sigh on her lips with a groan. His damp body stiffened against her, motionless, save the throb where their bodies were joined and the pounding beat of his heart.

He withdrew from her, dropping his head into the curve of her neck.

"I won't be givin' you a baby," he told her, his voice rough. Then with a grunt of pain, he released her to lay on his side.

Cool air breezed over her skin. "Is your arm all right?" she asked.

He released a pent-up breath. "Won't be tellin' Doc what set it to flamin' this time."

She rose on her elbow to look at him. His hair was damp and his skin glowed with perspiration. The sight of him made her chest ache. She gave herself the gift of running her palm over his slick flesh, leaned close to press her nose to the skin of his chest. "Might as well make use of all that water," she said.

Getting to her knees, she wrapped one of the towels they'd been lying on around her and tucked in the end to secure it.

He sat and wiped his forehead on his arm.

She let him get to his feet alone and watched him walk to the tub. She didn't have to think about anything more than this night. She refused to spoil any of it by considering the reality of her situation. She reached for her wrapper. "I'm going to run up and check on Tyler."

Jonas stepped into the tub and lowered himself into the water. "Still plenty warm."

"I'll be right back."

"Hope no other women come strollin' through that door while I'm waitin' for you."

"Take names. I'll invite them to my ladies' society."

He laughed, and she couldn't resist leaning over to kiss him before she left.

She let herself into their room and stood over Tyler, who slept peacefully. She adjusted the covers around his shoulders and kissed his hair. Her love for this boy kept her strong when life appeared bleak. That same love would give her the courage she needed to stick with her plan. Even though that plan meant giving up hope of anything more with Jonas.

A few minutes later, Eliza re-entered the room and locked the door. "He's sleeping like a rock."

Jonas's hair was slicked back and dripping, so with his freshly shaven face, every sculptured plane and angle was visible. His handsome appeal took her breath away.

"How's your arm?" she asked.

"Feels like I've been shot."

"Jonas." She knelt beside the tub.

"What?"

Impulsively, she pressed her cheek to his sleek, wet shoulder. He took care of her, he considered her feelings and her wishes, and those traits were dangerously seductive. He made her wish she could change what she had to do, and she couldn't let her resolve weaken.

"Somethin' wrong?" he asked.

She shook her head, but an empty ache expanded in her chest. He was strong, so kind and capable. She wanted to unburden her heart to him, wanted to share her fear and despair, but she couldn't. If he knew, he would want to fix it, and her situation couldn't be fixed. It could only be escaped.

"There's room," he urged. "C'mon."

She surveyed his sleek body under the shimmering water, taking only a second to decide. She wanted this time and this connection with Jonas. Once she was gone and years of living on her own stretched out ahead of her, she would have these moments to look back upon and treasure.

After producing pins from the pocket of her wrapper, she secured her hair, then draped the wrapper and towel over the chair and joined him. Water sloshed over the sides of the tub.

Unconcerned with the floor, he soaped a sponge and washed her shoulders, her legs, her feet. "Mighty pretty toes, too," he told her.

The degree of ease and security she felt with Jonas surprised her. She trusted him, and trust set her world right for now. The admiring way he looked at her brought tears to her eyes, so she hid them by rinsing her face, then quickly leaning to kiss him.

He took hold of her ankle and pulled her close, right onto his lap until their bodies fit together and she straddled him.

He returned the lazy kiss.

"Your arm," she objected.

"I'll rest it right here on the side. See?"

Another kiss, and another, and he laughed as more water hit the floor and soaked the towels. Jonas assured her his arm wasn't an issue this time, and it was another half hour before they dried and dressed and fled to his quarters. He stoked the fire in the fireplace and they sat close together on the patterned rug while their hair dried.

"Eliza Jane," he said, leaning to tuck a tendril of hair behind her ear. "It's probably a bad time…so soon after losin' Jenny and all…"

She covered his lips with her fingertips and made a shushing sound. "Don't say anything more," she begged. "Please. Not right now."

"But things need sayin'."

"Not now," she pleaded, her adoring gaze taking in the shadowed angles of his sculpted face, the distinct divot in his full upper lip. She wanted to remember the way he made her feel, the way he looked at her. "Please."

She took the hand he raised to her cheek and kissed each knuckle. The same hands that had won fistfights touched her with knee-weakening tenderness. He was a man of fascinating contrasts. His eyes betrayed reluctant acquiescence. He leaned forward to kiss her, and the kiss was tender and filled with emotion.

He gathered cushions and they lay before the warmth of the crackling fire and in the security of each other's arms until Eliza woke with a start.

She had drifted off to sleep. It couldn't have been for long, because the fire was still blazing. "I have to go," she told him.

He walked her to the door and kissed her, then followed her up the stairs and kissed her again. She left him standing in the hall in only his trousers.

Jonas stood outside the door a few minutes, and finally took the stairs down to his quarters. The fire still snapped in the grate and the cushions lay tossed about. The room was just as he'd left it, but now it felt lonely.

He rubbed the backs of his fingers over his smoothly shaven jaw, reliving the past hours. His arm throbbed. Until now he'd been too absorbed with Eliza Jane to pay notice to the pain. He hadn't been taking the medicine Doc had given him. He didn't like the groggy effects, and he sure didn't want to get dependent on it. Reading usually took his mind off the pain and made him sleepy.

He fashioned a comfortable spot on the divan with pillows and a blanket and picked up a journal, finding the page where he'd left off the night before.

He'd been reading so much that he'd become familiar with his father's accounts of Silver Bend's inhabitants, the way he twined weather reports with town events and patient calls, and how he shortened people's names to initials.

Jonas had worked his way through to details of the rainy spring of 1878, following a harsh winter. A debate over a proposed saloon and gaming hall had held the town council at odds. Most of the residents had been opposed. Seems they'd been concerned about attracting an unsavory element of clientele to their peaceful town. Others held out for the profit, but lost the vote. No wonder the people of Silver Bend had welcomed Jonas so eagerly upon his return.

A saloon guaranteed tax revenue, and he had assured them from the first that his establishment would be orderly and law-abiding and that no rooms would be rented to girls for the purpose of entertaining men.

"Old Jess hasn't recovered," his father had written, referring to the horse that had pulled his buggy for the previous ten years.

I've known for weeks that I need to do the humane thing and put him down, but I haven't had the heart for it.

Visits to the Sutherland home were mentioned so often that Jonas glanced over them, pausing when something caught his attention. A particular notation grabbed his interest.

A morning nap suits me this fine spring day. After several hours of waiting through the night, I delivered a healthy baby boy to E.J.S. at four o'clock this morning. She is doing well. J.L. insisted on being at her side. I was most concerned over J.L. throughout the ordeal. Any excitement makes her weak and short of breath and could be the thing that causes her heart to fail. I was firm that if she stayed in the room, she would lie down beside her sister.

Confused, Jonas went back and read the passage over again.

I delivered a healthy baby boy to E.J.S. at four o'clock this morning.

Clearly his father had been confused or drunk when he'd written this. EJS were Eliza Jane's initials. Jonas read back a ways, looking for clarification of the mistake, finding several references to visiting the Sutherland home, but none that would disprove those words.

So he read forward. A day later his father wrote of visiting the Sutherland house to check on the baby, then again a week later. Three weeks later, he made a call on EJS and pronounced her well.

Jonas let the information settle in his mind, but the settling caused copious upheaval in his thinking. His father had often used initials when writing about familiar townspeople, and though the man undoubtedly drank every night, his notes had never been anything but clear, precise records of his days.

If Jonas believed his father's writings and the pattern of well-recorded events, he would have to accept that Eliza Jane had given birth to a child.

He double-checked the day and year. Eight years ago on May 29. His mind tripped over that notation. Jonas went over the account books daily, so he was well aware of today's date. *Today* was May 29.

The very day they'd celebrated Tyler's birthday.

Facts that hadn't quite fit together and things he'd taken for granted shifted into place. If he was to believe this journal—and Jonas had no reason not to, since the journals were his father's personal diaries, and the man had never expected anyone to read them—then he had to believe Eliza Jane was Tyler's mother.

The fact certainly explained her devotion.

Jonas's previous knowledge of females had been gained with women of experience. Now that he thought back on it, perhaps this hadn't seemed like Eliza's first time. Her responses had been unpracticed and natural, but she hadn't been fearful. He'd been glad for that and for the fact that he hadn't hurt her.

Seems now there was a reason. Eliza Jane had been with a man before, and that man had fathered a child.

But as far as anyone knew, Tyler was Jenny Lee's son.

Jonas groaned inwardly at his lack of perception. The fact had been right there in front of him all along. Of course the boy wasn't Jenny's Lee's. All the descriptions of heart problems and weakness should have told Jonas that Jenny Lee had been too sick to carry and deliver a baby—*if* he'd been paying attention.

Eliza Jane's curious behavior around her brother-in-law swirled into focus. Royce knew the truth, and he was using his knowledge against her somehow.

Jonas got a sick feeling in his belly.

If Royce Dunlap was Tyler's father, then that meant Royce and Eliza Jane—

Jonas couldn't explore that. Uh-uh. No.

He thought of her expression and reaction the day that Luther fellow brought the note. Jonas recalled sitting at a nearby table and seeing Eliza Jane's demeanor around Royce. She was leery of him.

Now. But had she once loved him? Jonas tried to recall what he knew of the Sutherlands, but many of the events while he'd been away were only hearsay. He was sure that Royce and Jenny Lee had been married at least ten years back, so Eliza Jane and Royce couldn't have been courting eight years ago.

Royce had already been married. Had he forced himself on her? It wouldn't matter how long ago that had been, Jonas would probably have to kill him if he knew for sure.

Jonas skimmed forward, seeking mentions of the Sutherlands, finding only subsequent visits for Jenny Lee and later on for the infant Tyler.

Jonas grabbed the next ledger in the sequence and the next, thumbing through pages, passing a year. Two. Nothing answered his questions. Nowhere did he find a record of Jenny Lee giving birth to a child. And his father's reports were meticulous.

Finally, with his eyes burning, Jonas glanced at the Seth Thomas clock on the mantel, noted it was nearly morning, and convinced himself to turn down the lamp. The fire had dwindled, so he banked the ashes and climbed into bed.

By sheer force of will, he made himself close his eyes and relax his limbs. He'd broken his number one rule when it came to women. Fact was, since Eliza Jane had taken over his thoughts, he'd forgotten about the rule. He'd become emotionally involved.

And he liked the connection. He liked the way it felt to care about her. And nothing about their attraction had been one-sided, he was sure of that.

It was impossible not to think of what had taken place that evening. When he closed his eyes, he could see her, smell her, feel her touch and hear her soft sounds of pleasure. Jonas let himself drift off with those memories fresh in his mind.

Sometime later, he sat straight up in bed. "*I might not be here then,*" she'd said about his October birthday and the cake he'd requested. She was planning to run away and take Tyler with her.

That's why she needed a job and money. That's why she didn't want Royce to know what she was up to.

Royce was using Tyler against her somehow, Jonas was sure of it. Jonas had never had much use for the man, and his behavior continued to reinforce that opinion. Since Henry's death, the brick factory employees worked from dawn to dusk and their living conditions had declined. Royce withheld donations to the town that his father-in-law had always made. Jonas had no proof of what in tarnation had happened, but this situation with Eliza Jane didn't add up.

He turned over and punched his pillow. He should have taken the medicine after all.

Chapter Twelve

For the next several days, Eliza Jane blushed whenever their eyes met. He loved that about her, along with everything else, like the sheen of her hair in the sunlight and the soft feminine fragrance that clung to her. He'd decided to sit on the information he'd discovered. If he told her he knew, she might feel she couldn't trust him. Or she might fear he thought less of her, which couldn't have been more wrong. But he didn't want to chance it.

His every instinct was to take action. Go in with his fists raised and his feet planted. But he risked losing her, because exposure was exactly what she feared. He would rein in his anger and the need for answers and wait. He needed to see how things played out.

Several times while they were alone in the office, he looked up to find her studying him. Occasionally that week they shared heated kisses in the hallway. Twice he'd shoved a chair in front of the office door and she'd willingly come into his arms.

Jonas wondered what it would take to earn her trust, or if he ever could. She'd been disappointed by men, so the fact that she offered this bit of herself was already a concession on her part. But he had it bad for this woman.

On Friday, Jonas invited Eliza and Tyler on an outing and had a surprise planned for the following morning. Dressed in his usual trousers, shirt and felt hat, he showed up with a horse and buggy. As always, his revolver hung at his hip.

Tyler scrambled up while Jonas helped Eliza. "Where are we going?" he asked.

"You'll see soon enough. Enjoy the ride."

Eliza treasured the warm spring sun. She pointed to cascades of wild blue hyacinth flourishing on a rocky hillside. "Aren't they beautiful?"

"You can eat 'em in a pinch," Jonas remarked. "But that—" he pointed to foliage with tiny yellow petals growing in patches between sagebrush "—sagebrush buttercup is poisonous. Just a little will make you sick."

Purplish grass widows flourished on green hillsides and delicate fairy bells bordered a clear flowing stream.

"I haven't been out like this for a long time," Eliza told him.

Reins held loosely between his fingers, Stetson shading his eyes, he met her gaze over Tyler's head. "'Spect you needed to get out then."

"'Spect I did," she replied.

His grin flooded her heart with warmth. He was too much. Too good. She'd let her feelings leak beyond the parameters of emotional safety, and the knowledge made her uneasy.

"Once summer gets here, lupine and honeysuckle will take over the show on these hills," he told them.

Eventually, a cluster of buildings, barns and corrals came into view. Tyler pointed. "Is that where we're going?"

"Yup. See that pasture yonder?"

Tyler shaded his eyes with his small hand. "There's horses eating grass."

Jonas nodded. "One of 'em is Jeremiah."

"Oh, boy! Can I ride him?"

"Ever been on a horse?"

"Papa only has a carriage. I asked Mama before, and she said I could try it when I was bigger. Am I bigger enough?"

Jonas looked to Eliza, and she gave him a nod. "You can ride 'im," he said.

Tyler stood and let out a whoop that pierced their ears. Eliza took him by the arm and encouraged him back onto the seat before he toppled out of the buggy.

They pulled up near one of the barns, and a sun-darkened old fellow with worn leather suspenders over his faded shirt hobbled out.

"Land sakes, who'd you bring along?" he asked, with raised brows.

"Miss Sutherland and Tyler," Jonas replied, then to Eliza, "This here's Lilibelle's pa, Willie."

"How'do, miss."

"Pleased to meet you," she replied.

Tyler shot in front of her to make his way down, and she waited for Jonas to tie the reins to the brake handle and come around to assist her.

"I'll keep 'im safe," he assured her, as he settled her on the ground.

Jonas went into the barn for a harness. With Tyler on his heels, he strode past the corrals, climbed over a fence and whistled.

A horse with a coat as dark and shiny as the surface of strong coffee, galloped toward him. The animal drew up before Jonas, bobbing its head in recognition, and Jonas reached to pat its neck. The horse's mane and tail were black and wavy, the lower portions of its legs black, too.

Jonas rubbed the animal's neck, found a spot at the base of its mane and scratched it hard. "Watch this, Tyler. When I find a spot that feels good, his lips'll quiver."

Sure enough, the horse curled up its hairy upper lip, and it quivered. Jonas laughed. Tyler looked up at Eliza with a wide grin, then turned back to observe Jonas's every move.

Jonas showed him how to introduce himself to a horse that was unfamiliar with him. Tyler climbed on the bottom rung of the fence to watch as Jonas slipped the halter over the horse's head and led the animal through a gate and toward the barn. Then he leaped down and followed.

"I'll saddle 'im, and you can ride in the corral. He's not skittish, but just the same don't be whoopin' and hollerin' around animals you don't know, you hear?"

"Yes, sir."

"Some horses get scared at sounds or quick movements, and you don't know which horses those might be."

"Yes, sir."

Eliza trailed behind as Tyler dogged Jonas's steps, following him into the barn and listening as Jonas explained the tack and the procedure for placing it on the horse. The interior was warm and smelled of hay, oiled leather and animals.

"Are you gonna ride 'im, too?" Tyler asked.

"Not today. I exercise him once in a while, but this old boy's seen a lot of trail and too many battles. He's carried me while bullets flew around us, and he's stood overnight in the freezin' wind and snow for plenty of winters. I figure he's got only easy days comin' to 'im."

"He's real pretty," Tyler said.

"Handsome," Jonas corrected with a chuckle as he buckled the saddle under Jeremiah's belly. "He's a Salerno. His breed comes from Italy. Has Spanish and Arabian blood in 'im."

"Do they have more at Italy? Maybe I can get one."

Jonas kept a straight face. "Italy's a country across the ocean, and Jeremiah himself didn't come from there. Just his ancestors did."

"Maybe Jeremiah can have a baby an' I can get *him*."

"Jeremiah's a gelding." Jonas's patience as he explained the subject so the boy could understand touched Eliza. She listened to his soothing voice with as much interest as Tyler.

Sun streamed though the open barn doors, creating a white-gold rectangle of light that illuminated the lustrous animal, the broad-shouldered man, and the boy who listened intently with his sun-gilded head tilted to the side. Dust motes danced in the air, creating an ethereal picture framed by the shaded and ordinary world.

As Jonas stroked the horse, spoke to the boy and occasionally shared an amused look with her, Eliza realized with resounding awe that she was in love.

Unquestionably, heart-in-her-throat crazy for Jonas Black.

Every inch of her being confirmed it: the knot in her chest; the flutter of her heart; the bittersweet ache that brought the sting of tears to her eyes and took her breath away. The youthful feelings she'd had for Forest paled in comparison to the passion she felt for Jonas.

She should never have let this happen.

She would never forget this moment.

How could she live a day without him?

By the time her heart had settled back to a normal rhythm, Jonas was helping Tyler onto Jeremiah's back. Jonas took the reins and led them outside.

Eliza stood in the shade at the corner of the barn and watched as Jonas walked the horse and Tyler beamed from ear to ear.

"Look, Aunt Liza! Look at me!"

She waved, then stood with her fingers laced.

"Fine boy, your nephew," Willie Grimshaw said from beside her, catching her attention.

She found her voice. "Yes. He is."

"My Lily told me your sister passed on. My sympathies to you."

"Thank you."

"Do you know the fella riding behind you?"

She arranged her thoughts to figure out what he'd asked. "Someone was behind us?"

"Stopped yonder by that outcropping of rock to the west. Stayed there when you came on to the ranch, then rode off."

"No," she answered. "I didn't see him."

Willie limped toward the fence and leaned against it, thumbing his hat back on his head.

Eliza found a worn stump used as a mounting step and settled on it to watch the remainder of Tyler's ride. Eventually, Jonas had to convince the child it was time to let the horse go back to his pasture, promising him they would return.

One of the ranch hands brought them a pail of water and tin cups before they headed back.

"Did you know someone was behind us on our way here?" she asked Jonas when Tyler ran ahead to climb into the buggy.

"Saw 'im," Jonas replied.

"Did you see who it was?"

"Too far out to say."

They reached the buggy and Jonas helped her up to the seat.

Jonas recently being shot was fresh in her mind. "Do you think we're being followed?"

The possibility of a shooting while Tyler was along struck terror into her heart. Jonas must have recognized it, because he said, "Willie shouldn't've said anything. Most likely a coincidence."

Tyler could talk of nothing but the horse and his ride all the way home and for the rest of the day. Eliza couldn't shake the thought of a stranger following them.

Jonas joined them at supper in the dining room, and still the child chattered on about Jeremiah and his hopes for a horse of his own. She'd never seen him so animated or happy. Having Jonas's attention and guidance brought out a side of him Eliza had never seen.

Every once in a while she forgot herself and imagined for a moment what their lives could be like with Jonas. But then reality loomed and she heard Royce's threats and saw his glare. He had the power to expose her indiscretion to the world.

She could handle that, and she would if she thought putting an end to the deception would be her solution. She could live with the taint. It was what Royce could do to Tyler that paralyzed her. And since Royce couldn't care less about him, he wouldn't hesitate. If he exposed the fact that Tyler was her child out of wedlock, Tyler would be ridiculed and ostracized by adults and classmates alike. He would have to make a choice between being an outcast in the town where he'd been born or leaving in shame. She'd always known the possibility was there. Always wanted to protect him. Taking him away was bad enough, but at least he didn't have to learn the truth in a completely humiliating manner.

Ever since she'd known he was growing inside her, she'd loved and shielded him. When Forest had run off, she'd been forced to do the only thing that would save Tyler shame. She'd given him a mother and a father.

Jonas finished his coffee and set down his cup. He raised one dark eyebrow and mouthed the word, "Pie?"

Smiling, she shook her head. "You and Tyler have a slice."

"A slice of what?" Tyler asked.

"As soon as those parsnips are gone, you can have a piece of Lilibelle's apple pie."

He wrinkled his nose. "Do I gotta eat all of 'em?"

She nodded.

Nadine was serving in the dining room that evening, and she came past to pour Jonas more coffee and offer Eliza tea.

"Thank you, yes," Eliza replied.

"And we'll have a couple man-size slices o' pie," Jonas added.

Eliza glanced at Tyler's empty plate. He grinned at her. For some reason, she was drawn to look at Jonas. He simply gave her a nonchalant smile.

Nadine was picking up their dirty dishes.

"I'll be out with your tea and dessert," Nadine said and walked toward the kitchen.

Eliza looked from Tyler to Jonas and back. She suspected Jonas had eaten those parsnips when she hadn't been looking. Tyler had never eaten that particular vegetable so fast in his short life. But she hadn't qualified that he must actually *eat* them, only that the buttered vegetables had to be gone, she realized. "Just so you know, I'm aware that Jonas ate those parsnips. Next time I'll be more careful in my instructions."

Tyler's gaze shot to Jonas and they shared a look she couldn't decipher.

Once the males had finished their desserts, Jonas excused himself to head over to the Silver Star and she took Tyler upstairs. She didn't know how many "next times" were in store for them. With sad-sweet awareness, she acknowledged that Tyler was as taken with the man as she.

The next several days passed much too quickly, but the nights stretched into eternity. Each night Eliza lay in their dark hotel room only feet from her boy and listened to the sound of his breathing. Too much time to think. Too much time to explore regrets and hopeless dreams. She'd given away her baby. She'd relinquished her maternal rights to spare him because she loved him so much. Every time she'd heard him call Jenny Lee "Mama," a needle of agony had pierced her heart.

Jenny's limitations and need for help had been both a blessing and a private torture. Eliza had been able to bathe him, feed him, care for him and eventually walk him to and from school. Doing so was a privilege.

Tonight she thought of Moses in the Bible, who was raised as the queen's son, but nursed and cared for by his own mother. Her own situation wasn't nearly as noble, however. The predicament had been brought on by her impetuousness and foolish trust.

Jenny had told Eliza again and again what an amazing gift she'd given her. She'd been so thankful and it had pleased her so to call Tyler her own. Royce had gone along without resistance. Eliza suspected anything that kept Jenny pacified made it easier for him to work his subterfuge behind the scenes without too many inquiries.

Eliza's father had been much the same way with Jenny. Their parents babied and mollified her. Jenny and Eliza each owned a percentage of the company, because Sutherland Brick had started out with Eliza Jane's mother's money, and her mother had chosen the recipients of the holdings.

Eliza's father had built the business from the ground up. Later on, Eliza had invested, and their money had gone from income and savings to working for them and multiplying.

Jenny hadn't cared in the least about the company or the money. Her world had been confined to her rooms and the people she loved.

Sometimes Eliza wondered what would have happened if Forest had stayed. If he had married her, and they'd raised Tyler as their own. Would she have remained at the factory or would she still have quit to care for Jenny? In any case, she'd be able to claim Tyler. He would call *her* Mama.

She might have even had more children.

Oh, she was a foolish woman for giving rein to the what-ifs, but the nights were unbearably long.

A soft rap sounded on the door.

Eliza's heart skittered. She folded back the covers

and reached for her satin dressing gown on the foot of the bed. Slipping it on, she padded to the door.

Jonas's broad-shouldered frame and tousled dark hair were outlined by the gas lamp on the wall behind him. "Come to my room," he whispered.

Her body responded with a tingle of warmth and a rush of blood through her veins. "I can't stay long," she whispered in return. "Wait a moment."

She turned into the room, covered her child snugly and picked up the key.

In the hall, Jonas took the key from her and locked the door. Taking her hand, he led her down the back stairway. In his sitting room, he'd prepared a fire and opened a bottle of sherry. He poured them each a snifter and handed her one.

Eliza brought it to her lips hesitantly. She took a sip of the pale tangy liquid. The flavor was strong and citrus-sweet with a nutty taste like almonds. "It's good."

Jonas led her to the coverlet he'd lain out and took the glass from her to set it aside.

Without speaking, he reached for her gown and undressed her. After shrugging out of his shirt, he knelt before her, cupped her hips and pressed kisses against her abdomen.

Eliza threaded her fingers into his hair and closed her eyes. She wanted to remember every touch, every kiss, every sound and whisper and moment of their brief time together. Tears seeped from the corners of her eyes, and she swiped them away quickly before kneeling to face him.

He rested his palm along her cheek and gazed into her eyes.

Eliza's contrary heart wept with the keen adoration she felt for this man she could never have, for the love she could never declare or allow.

"When I look at you durin' the day," he told her, "I think about you like this. In my arms. Under me with your black hair in a tumble. Your lips red from kissin'."

His words, plain as they were, were poetry and music to her empty soul, a soul that had yearned for recognition and acceptance. His praise brought a lump to her throat.

"Just the lovin' part isn't enough," he said. "I want you to belong to me."

"Don't," she said around the constriction, and shook her head and lowered it so he wouldn't see the regret and shame washing over her.

He lifted her chin on a knuckle so their eyes met. "Don't be ashamed. What I feel for you is decent and honorable."

"Oh, Jonas, I don't doubt your honor for a moment. You're the finest man I've ever known."

"Then tell me what's holdin' you back. Tell me."

"It's nothing you could change," she said. "I'm here now, and we have tonight. I know it's unfair, but this is all I have to give. Wanting you is wrong, but I can't stop."

He pulled her into his arms and held her tightly. "I don't want you to stop."

He worked his magic with his hands and his kisses,

and Eliza gave back with her whole heart, hoping to show him he was everything to her, wanting to assure him of her desire and her need for him.

He was tender one moment, demanding and urgent the next, the heat and his passion surprising her. His fervent dedication to her pleasure and comfort brought more tears to her eyes. And he was still taking care of her, carefully protecting her by not planting his seed in her.

Eliza wanted to cry, but feared if she started she'd never stop, and she didn't want him to think he'd displeased her in any way, because he hadn't. She was the one who didn't measure up. She was the one holding back. She didn't deserve his esteem.

The mantel clock chimed, and Eliza grabbed up her robe. "I have to go."

He said nothing, but raised to a sitting position and grabbed his trousers, reaching into a pocket and producing her key.

She took it from him. "I'll let myself out."

He didn't argue, and she was glad. She was nearly to the door when he spoke. "Sleep well, Eliza Jane."

She slipped out and ran silently up the stairs, managing to unlock the door and let herself in before the tears came. Eliza ran to her bed and huddled under the covers, holding her pillow to catch her sobs.

She closed her eyes against the memory of the question he'd asked so concernedly that first time, but it rang in her mind. *"Did I hurt you?"*

She cried until she feared she'd wake Tyler, so she

calmed herself, turned the damp side of her pillow under and arranged the covers. She wasn't ashamed of loving Jonas, nor was she ashamed that she'd loved Forest. But she'd been hurt and humiliated.

Her chest ached with a stab of regret and an entirely different kind of shame. Forest had left her without so much as a by-your-leave. Left her to wait and wonder as the days and weeks and months stretched out.

She was planning to do the same thing to Jonas.

He wanted a commitment. If she hadn't silenced him every time he'd tried, he would have proposed by now. But he was honoring her wishes. Loving her the only way she'd let him.

Too late she'd discovered a man who appreciated her and held her in high esteem. There was no way anything could come of their growing feelings for each other. And no way she could deny herself the pleasure she found in his arms.

She would never sleep well again.

Eliza hoped she'd masked her sleepless night by rinsing her face with cold water and by liberal applications of witch hazel, massage cream and a dusting of rice powder. She served Tyler breakfast and he sat at the end of a table with Matt, Daniel and Phoebe. Eliza fixed a plate and nibbled at the eggs and a slice of ham.

Watching Tyler interact with the Harper boys, she was sure staying here had been a good experience for him. He'd been able to stretch beyond his usual confines and participate in things a boy should. Jonas's attention had brought an enormous change to Tyler's confidence. She wouldn't regret the experience.

The boys finished and carried their plates to the kitchen. Tyler returned, grabbed up his books and his sack lunch. "Bye, Aunt Liza."

"Have a good day," she told him with a smile.

At night he kissed and hugged her before bed, but here in front of the boys, he acted too old for that.

The three of them jostled each other, seeing who could get out the door first, and the sound of their laughter and running echoed in the back hall.

"Shame they grow up to be men," Phoebe said with a teasing grin. "They're still so cute at his age."

"I heard that," Ward said on his way to the kitchen.

Eliza finished her tea and took her dishes into the other room, where Lilibelle was giving orders for the day.

When Eliza reached the office, Jonas was already seated at his desk, a mug of coffee within reach. He held a small pouch in his right hand and squeezed it repeatedly. "Doc told me to work my hand and arm with this bag of sand," he told her, then tossed it down. "Sleep well?"

Visions of their lovemaking the night before brought heat to her collar and made her heart trip. His sly expression told her he knew exactly what she was thinking.

The small room seemed to close in on her. If there had been a window, she would have opened it. "Did you?"

"Not particularly."

She sat, arranged the pen and ink on the blotter and

opened one of the ledgers he'd stacked there. "What's first?"

The day passed unremarkably. Jonas left to attend a meeting with the town council members and returned after lunch.

Eliza checked her brooch, and when it was time for the boys to return from school, she went to the kitchen and prepared them slices of bread and butter and poured cold buttermilk.

Ada arrived and they sat together at the table, waiting.

Lilibelle and the kitchen help worked their dinner magic around them. Eliza and Ada chatted. Finally, Ada stood. "What do you suppose those boys have found to occupy them for so long? They know chores are waitin'."

"I'll go check," Eliza told her, making her way out the rear door that led into the alley and headed west behind the dry goods store. She walked all the way to the schoolhouse and found the door standing open.

Miss Fletcher was erasing the blackboards when Eliza entered the classroom. She turned with a greeting. "Well, hello, Miss Sutherland. What brings you here?"

"Tyler and the Harper boys haven't come home yet, and I thought they might still be in class for some reason."

Frowning, the teacher brushed her hands together. "Tyler, Daniel and Matthew weren't in class today. I thought they'd all come down with something."

Eliza absorbed the teacher's words. "They never came to school?"

Miss Fletcher shook her head. "No."

Chapter Thirteen

The boys had never arrived at school?

"What?" Panic rising, Eliza turned back toward the door. "I don't understand. Ada and I sent them out at the usual time."

The teacher gave a disapproving shake of her head. "You might look at the nearest fishing hole. It's a bright spring day, and even the finest of students has been known to be lured away by the weather."

"Tyler doesn't know the first thing about fishing," she answered, hurrying from the small building.

Eliza ran the entire way back to the hotel and burst into the kitchen. "They never went to school!"

Ada got up from the table. "You're sure?"

"Miss Fletcher said they didn't arrive this morning. She thought maybe they went fishing."

"Daniel and Matt know I'd skin them alive if they played hooky," Ada said, hands on hips.

"But maybe?" Eliza asked.

Ada raised both hands and tilted her head. "Maybe."

Eliza hurried back to the office, but Jonas wasn't there. This time of the afternoon he sometimes spent a couple of hours at the saloon. She ran out the front door and along the boardwalk. Out of breath, she pushed open the green batwing doors.

Jonas sat at a table with Quay and two women dressed in plain skirts and shirtwaists. One of them Eliza recognized as Madeline Holmes. "Somethin' wrong?" Jonas asked after one look at her.

"Tyler and the Harper boys didn't go to school this morning. Miss Fletcher said she hadn't seen them all day. She thought maybe they found a fishing hole." Her mind ran through worse possibilities. "What if they found one of those poisonous snakes and it bit them?"

"Wouldn't bite all three of 'em at the same time." Always logical, Jonas got to his feet. "Someone could've run back for help if one got bit. Most likely they're fishin'."

"Do you know where?"

"I can figure it out. Would he try to find Willie's place so he could see the horse again?"

She pressed a knuckle against her lips as she considered. "It doesn't sound like him, but he's never missed school before, either."

Quay stood. "I'll saddle our horses, boss," he said on his way out the door.

"Rowena," Jonas said, turning to the red-haired woman across the table. "Go find Marshal Haglar and let 'im know we're lookin' for Tyler and Ada's boys, will you?"

"Sure thing." She rose and headed for the door.

"Are there any other places Tyler would go?" Jonas asked. "Home maybe?"

"Possibly," Eliza replied. "But there's no one there. Royce is only home overnight."

"Why don't you go check, just in case?"

She nodded. "I'll have to find my key. I'm sure Royce will have the house locked."

"Maddie, you go with her, will ya?"

The woman nodded and joined Eliza as she headed for the door. Eliza's thoughts were too scattered to make much sense, but she fervently prayed they would reach the house and find all three boys. She didn't know why she had such a bad feeling pressing down on her.

The dark-haired woman accompanied her as Eliza used the key and unlocked the front door, entering the familiar foyer.

"Tyler?" she called. Her voice seemed to echo. She called again.

They performed a diligent search. Without comment, Maddie took in the high-ceilinged rooms and quality furnishings.

"They haven't been here," Eliza said.

Nora called to Eliza as she walked down the front stairs. "Eliza Jane! It's so good to see you!"

"Tyler didn't show up for school today," Eliza told her in a rush. "I was hoping he might have come here. He's with two other boys."

"I haven't seen anyone," Nora told her, concern creasing her brow.

They stood on the front walk. Eliza glanced at the houses across the street. "Jonas has gone to check fishing holes. I suppose it couldn't hurt to ask around until he gets back."

"We'll join you," Nora said. The three of them canvassed the entire block, enlisting the help of Marian Atwell and a couple other neighbors.

Back on the street in front of her childhood home, Eliza gazed south toward the brickyard where the three-story main structure, the smokestacks and drying sheds beyond were visible. Tyler had only been there a few times. She couldn't imagine him going for any reason.

As they headed back toward the saloon, Maddie tucked her arm through Eliza's. "They're going to find your boy."

"I've never raised a hand to that child." Eliza's voice shook. "But he's going to get a willow whip across his backside for this one."

Ada came out of the hotel, her earlier vexation gone and disbelief setting in. "I've looked everywhere I know of," she said.

Eliza shared where they'd searched, and then took Ada's cold hand and they continued on to the saloon, where the marshal was waiting.

Ada took a chair at a table by herself. Eliza paced the worn oak floor, checking the windows every few minutes.

At last Jonas and Quay returned without the boys. Jonas's mouth showed his grim decision. "Time we let Royce know and organize a search."

A new fear settled in Eliza's heart. She glanced at Ada to see shock registering as the seriousness of the situation became clearer.

The marshal motioned for attention and assigned jobs. "Quay, head to the brickyard and alert the boy's father. Tell him to have his employees search every inch of that place. Jonas, go get Yale and Silas, anyone else you can find. We'll work our way through town first, then if we have to, we'll spread outward."

Within minutes every available person was searching storage rooms, outbuildings, yards and all the possible nooks and crannies. Eliza sat beside Ada and patted her arm to comfort her, though she wasn't feeling very confident at that moment.

Royce arrived at the saloon and made a production out of asking questions. He came to sit beside Eliza. "How are you holding up, dear?"

Eliza straightened in the chair. She didn't want to look at him. She hated that he had any part in her and Tyler's lives, and she resented him being there, especially since his behavior was a calculated performance.

Bonnie brought kettles, and she and Maddie made tea.

"Drink this, dear," Bonnie told Eliza. "Tea always makes you feel better."

Eliza knew her friend was trying to be helpful, so she forced her shaking hands to pick up the cup. Inside she wanted to scream. Ada just sat and stared at the doorway.

"We're going to get to the bottom of this, you'll see," Royce said as though he was actually doing something to make that happen. Eliza finally looked at him because she couldn't believe his duplicity. He gave her what looked like an encouraging smile, but was really his way of gloating about the power he held over her. She wanted to hit him with something.

Another fifteen minutes passed before a commotion sounded in the street. Royce got up and met the men coming through the door with two boys between them. Daniel and Matt Harper's dirty faces were streaked with dried tears.

Ada got up and rushed to grab and hug them.

"Where's Tyler?" Eliza asked, pushing forward.

"Don't know," Dan replied, his youthful voice breaking.

Jonas held up several pieces of rope that had been sliced. "Found 'em tied up in the shed on Oak Street south of the church."

"What happened?" Ada asked.

Matt burst into tears and wrapped himself against his mother. She held him and looked to Daniel.

"We was headin' for school just like always," he told her, his voice animated. "We only got as far as behind the dry goods store and was walking by a wagon, and next thing I knowed, I heard scufflin'. I turned back and saw Matt's feet. Someone was dragging him 'round back of the wagon. Tyler was lyin' on the ground. I started toward 'em and somebody grabbed me and held an awful smellin' rag over my nose.

"Next thing I remember, me and Matt was tied up in that shed and Tyler wasn't there."

Eliza needed to throw up. She turned, spotted a wooden bucket at the end of the bar and ran for it. She retched until her eyes watered and she thought her stomach would turn inside out.

"I'll take care of this," Royce said, placing his hand on her shoulder. "Don't you worry." He turned and addressed the gathering in a loud voice. "I'll pay a reward of three hundred dollars to the man who brings my son back to me safe and sound."

Eliza collapsed to a sitting position on the floor. Maddie brought her a wet rag. "Here. Wipe your face, Miss Sutherland."

Jonas couldn't bear the look of fear on Eliza Jane's white face. It took all his gumption not to go pick her up and hold her till she stopped shaking. A display like that would draw speculation, and his time would be better spent finding Tyler.

"Sounds like somebody chloroformed 'em, but only took the Sutherland boy," Warren Haglar said quietly to the men who waited at the door for directions.

"Might be they'll get a ransom note," Yale suggested. "Dunlap has more money'n most in these parts."

"Jonas, you're probably the best tracker we've got," the marshal said.

Jonas had to pull his gaze away from Eliza being comforted by her brother-in-law. He couldn't be as effective as he needed to be if he let himself think of what this was doing to her or if he gave too much consideration to Tyler's fear.

His army days had involved more shooting than

tracking. He wasn't as skilled as he'd need to be, so he was going to have to be determined and diligent. Tyler and Eliza needed him, and he couldn't let them down.

"I'll check the roads out of town," he told the marshal. "That was early this mornin'. No tellin' how many horses and wagons traveled in and out since then."

"I know," Warren replied. "But we have to start somewhere."

The men looked at each other and Jonas knew what each of them was thinking. If Tyler was alive right now—and Jonas had to believe he was—he was terrified.

Satisfied to see that Maddie and Bonnie were looking after Eliza and Ada, he headed for the door. "Best not waste any more daylight."

As he'd feared, the tracks in and out of town were so numerous that no one set was clear enough to follow. Their options narrowed to spreading out and searching roads, fields, outlying farms and ranches.

Silas Bowers rode with Jonas. They searched east of town, walking their horses along streambeds, up rocky hillsides and through ravines. The enormity of the countryside and the length of time since Tyler had disappeared overwhelmed Jonas. He tried not to think of the limitless ways the boy could have come to harm. If someone wanted him dead, he'd had all the time and space he'd needed.

Jonas thought about the times he'd spent with him, remembered Tyler's childish perspective and inquisitive mind, and couldn't conceive of anyone wanting to hurt him.

Being the one left behind with his mother, Jonas had missed much of his own childhood. Tyler reminded him what it was like to look at life through innocent eyes.

The sky grew dark. He and Silas took out the jerky that Quay had given them and chewed it as they reluctantly turned back toward town.

Jonas hated to go back empty-handed. He dreaded seeing the look on Eliza Jane's face. Letting her down when she needed him stuck in his craw.

"Mebbe someone's found him by now," Silas said.

"Maybe," Jonas answered with more hope than conviction.

The lights of the saloon were ablaze, but no music came from inside when they tied their mounts out front.

Jonas pushed the doors aside and entered the building.

Eliza looked up from where she sat at a table with Madeline and Bonnie. She stood and watched him approach. "Nothing?" she asked.

"Too dark to keep lookin'," he replied.

There it was, the look that cut him to the quick.

"I'm raising the reward to five hundred dollars," Royce announced from across the room. "Whoever brings my boy home gets cash."

Jonas held Eliza's tortured gaze. Putting a price on her child's head made him seem like a possession, and he felt his temperature rise.

"Lilibelle's been cooking," Rowena told Jonas. "There's food at the hotel for the men who've been out."

"Did *she* eat?" he asked, indicating Eliza with a nod.

Rowena shook her head.

"Why don't you bring us meals?" he suggested.

"Right away." Rowena got up and hurried out the door.

"You're going to eat while my boy's out there somewhere?" Royce asked. "At the hands of a thief or a murderer?"

Eliza Jane's eyes closed against his words.

"We don't know that for sure," the marshal said.

"It's too dark to look anymore tonight," Jonas told him. "Won't help to risk horses, and it won't help for us to go hungry."

"Maybe you can sell tickets to this sideshow, Black," Royce said, walking closer.

Jonas just looked at him.

"Maybe you staged it to bring in business."

"What the hell are you talkin' about?" Jonas asked, already tired, hungry, and now mad. "Looks to me like we're losin' business here tonight. Anybody buyin' drinks?" he called to Quay.

"Sold a couple beers is all."

"And Lily's givin' away meals at the hotel," Jonas added.

"No one wants your charity," Royce spat out. "I can take care of my own family."

"Yeah, I've seen how well you do that," Jonas remarked.

"What's that mean?"

"When's Tyler's birthday?" Jonas asked.

"Jonas, don't," Eliza Jane said in a warning tone.

Royce was standing directly in front of Jonas now. He glanced at Eliza and back. "What difference does it make?"

Jonas was good and riled now. "Seems a man should know when his boy's birthday is. Make an effort to wish him well."

"I have a business to run," Royce told him. "A *respectable* business. The operation of the brickyard consumes my time. Unlike you, I don't make my living renting rooms to whores and running a slave trade on the side."

A tense silence fell over the room.

All eyes turned to Jonas.

Chapter Fourteen

"Which one of these women are you callin' a whore, Dunlap?" Jonas asked, reaching to unfasten his gun belt. "'Cause I'd love to plant my fist in your face on their behalf."

One of the bystanders took Jonas's holster and backed away.

A look of fear finally crossed Royce's face.

"C'mon." Jonas egged him on with a beckoning motion of his fingers and moved closer. "Which one?"

"This is precisely what I'd expect of you," Royce said, adjusting his already-perfect collar and tie and taking a step back. "A low-class threat from a two-bit—"

Royce didn't get the sentence finished because Jonas popped him in the jaw and sent him reeling backward onto a table, where he landed solidly, tipping it, and then slid to the floor.

"Marshal!" Royce called, getting to his knees with as much dignity as possible. "Are you going to stand there and let this one-horse mudsill pile on the agony when I already have all I can handle with finding my son?"

Warren stepped in front of Jonas. "I know you're a big bug in this town, but you got *some* pumpkins," he said to Royce. "Comin' in here and belittling the very man and the people who are lookin' for your boy. I ain't seen you out lookin'."

"I think you're forgetting who hired you," Royce said with an angry glare.

"The council hired 'im," Jonas pointed out.

"And the council can fire him just as easily." Royce got to his feet, but was none too steady on them. He gripped his jaw and worked it left and right, then opened and shut his mouth. A tiny rivulet of blood trickled from the corner and made a bright red dot on his starched white collar. Another spot appeared beside the first.

Eliza Jane took a few steps closer. She looked from one man to the other. "Nothing matters but getting Tyler home safely," she bit out. "Everyone's worried and tired, but you don't see the rest of us insulting each other or getting into fisticuffs at the end of a dreadful day."

She was angry and frightened, and color had risen in her cheeks. "Eat, for heaven's sake. Get some rest. But stop behaving like ruffians."

Jonas was still angry enough to beat Royce Dunlap into a fine paste, but also glaringly aware that Eliza saw his impulsive behavior as reprehensible. He nodded. "My apologies."

Rowena had shown up with a covered tray. She placed it on a table and nodded at him.

Silas sat and helped himself to a plate of savory roast and herbed potatoes. Maddie urged Eliza to take a plate. Once she did, Jonas seated himself across from her.

Rowena brought the men coffee and Bonnie supplied Eliza with another cup of tea. Royce finally took a seat near the door.

"Everybody needs some sleep," the marshal said. "We'll meet in front of my office and head out at first light."

Jonas hated that he couldn't comfort Eliza Jane publicly. He became aware of how secretive their relationship truly was and how damaging it could be for her to have it discovered.

"I don't think you should be alone tonight," Jonas said to her.

She looked up, her eyes filled with worry and a deep sadness. "If it is ransom they want, they won't hurt him. But then why haven't we heard anything yet?"

"I don't know," he answered, wishing he had the answers, or at the very least the opportunity to comfort her. "Maddie could stay with you. Or one of the others if you'd rather."

She nodded. "I like Maddie."

Jonas spoke to the other woman, and she was more than willing to keep Eliza Jane company that night. The two women headed for the hotel.

Royce left a short time later.

Jonas remained and poured pitchers of beer to share

with the men who'd stayed. The mood was subdued, the Silver Star uncharacteristically void of music and laughter.

Well after midnight, he locked the doors and went home. He stood on the boardwalk for ten or fifteen minutes, looking up at the night sky, finding the Big Dipper and swallowing down his unease. Somewhere a frightened little boy was away from his "mother" for the first time.

Jonas's father had been absent during his childhood, and Tyler sure deserved better than that. Jonas didn't have much experience praying, but he pleaded with the heavens for Tyler to still be alive and for him to be returned to them safely.

A wolf howled in the distance.

Eliza would never sleep until she knew Tyler was safe. Maddie had fallen asleep on the other side of the bed, and Eliza was grateful for her presence. Hundreds of sickening scenarios swam through her head, each more grisly than the last.

Though she couldn't truly comprehend the fact, someone had deliberately taken her child. From Daniel's description, the person had likely used chloroform on a cloth and sedated all three boys so he could get them out of the alley behind the hotel and dry goods store without a tussle. They'd probably been moved in the wagon that Daniel and Matt recalled sitting back there. No one in the businesses remembered a delivery or pickup that early.

At this point, she would almost be relieved to see a ransom note. Knowing a reason would be *something*.

Head throbbing, eyes dry, she woke after only an hour or so of sleep. She felt guilty for sleeping at all while Tyler was somewhere unknown, possibly hurt, undoubtedly terrified. It was still dark, but she lit a match and looked at her brooch. It would be light soon.

"Did you sleep?" Maddie asked.

"A little."

"I'll go get water," Maddie told her, giving Eliza a few minutes of privacy.

The hotel was already waking up by the time they were washed and dressed. Doors opened and closed and muffled voices could be heard from below.

Three successive cracks of gunfire caught Eliza's attention on her way down to the front foyer. She ran the rest of the way down the stairs. Boot heels sounded and Jonas shot out of the dining room, followed by several other men dressed for riding. The kitchen helpers showed up to learn what was going on, too.

Eliza followed as Jonas drew his revolver and threw open the front door. He hurried out across the porch and down the stairs.

"Stay back!" he called over his shoulder.

She stood on the porch and strained to see in the dim morning light.

"He's got the boy!" someone shouted from farther down Main Street toward the bank and the jail.

Eliza heard only those words and shot down the stairs, running full out in an effort to catch up with Jonas.

Chapter Fifteen

Doors opened along the street, several of the store owners who lived above or behind their shops having been awakened. As they passed the bank, the sun broke over the horizon, casting Main Street, the buildings and the inhabitants in a pinkish glow.

A man sat on a horse in front of the jail. The marshal rode up from the direction of his home on Second Street just in time to witness the gathering. Luther Vernon waited atop the horse without climbing down.

The horse shied and shifted its hind end around, bringing into Eliza's view the pale-haired child sitting in front of him.

"Tyler!" she shrieked.

Tyler turned his whole upper body and spotted her running at them, skirts flying. "Aunt Liza!"

Luther Vernon gripped Tyler under the arms, working the boy's legs over the saddle horn, and then leaned sideways to lower him to the ground.

Jonas got there first and caught the boy, easing his descent. Tyler had eyes only for Eliza as she reached him and fell to her knees, a joyful cry bursting from her throat. She grasped him to her breast and held him as tightly as she could, feeling the tremble in his slender frame and the rapid beat of his heart against hers.

Her son was safe and alive and in her arms. Never had she been more grateful or relieved. Never had she wanted to laugh and cry and burst apart with relief all at the same time. She held his face between her hands and kissed his eyes and cheeks, used her hem to wipe tears and dirt from them, and told him she loved him.

"Where'd you find 'im?" the marshal asked.

"Searched along Yakima Ridge. Found him behind some huckleberries, tied to a tree." Luther reached into a saddlebag. "Here's the rope."

Marshal Haglar took it and looked it over. "Looks like the same hemp that the Harper boys were tied with."

"I want the reward," Luther said. "Risked my neck for it."

"Take that up with Dunlap," the marshal told him.

The crowd parted and Royce stepped from the board-walk into the street. "You found my son?"

"There he is," Luther told him.

Royce turned and looked at Eliza. "Good thing someone was out looking instead of sleeping."

At the sound of his voice, Tyler turned in Eliza's arms and spotted Royce. "Papa!"

Royce walked forward, and Eliza released Tyler,

who hugged the man around the waist. Royce patted his head awkwardly. Eliza had the impression that he would brush off his jacket once no one was looking.

"Come with me to the bank," Royce called to Luther. "You'll have your reward money immediately."

Luther slid from the horse and tied it at the post in front of the jail. Royce said something to Tyler before turning away from him, and the two men headed for the bank.

Jonas stood watching Tyler with an undecipherable expression on his face, then met Eliza's gaze. She read suspicion and displeasure in his eyes. Jonas had recognized Royce's lack of emotion or concern. He strode to Tyler and hunkered down. "Marshal's gonna take you on over to his office and ask you some questions. After you talk a spell, you can go back to the hotel with your aunt."

"Can she come with us to the marshal's?"

"You bet." He nodded at Eliza, and she reached for Tyler's hand.

Tyler glanced up. "You comin', too?"

"Right behind you."

Inside the small office, Eliza took a chair and pulled Tyler onto her lap and pressed her face to the back of his head. He smelled of outdoors and maybe a little like horse and sweat. She didn't want to let go.

His telling of the events sounded pretty much like Daniel and Matt's, except Tyler told them he'd been kept blindfolded and tied in some kind of tiny structure. He'd been given food and water and then hauled onto a horse again, and left alone out of doors.

"Were you cold?" she asked.

"Uh-uh. The man covered me with a blanket and then later he took it away."

Jonas hunkered down in front of Tyler. "Are you hurt anywhere?"

Tyler opened both arms outward, and at first Eliza thought he was reaching for Jonas, but when Tyler pushed his wrist under Jonas's nose, his intent became plain.

Jonas took Tyler's forearm and gently eased back his sleeve, exposing raw chafe marks. The other wrist was the same.

"Doc will fix those right up for ya." Jonas's voice seemed gruffer than usual. He tousled Tyler's hair and got to his feet without looking at Eliza.

"You can take 'im home now, Miss Sutherland," the marshal told her.

Home had come to mean the safety of the hotel, and she couldn't wait to get her boy there.

"I'll come see you shortly," Jonas told her. "I'll send Doc over."

She nodded and led Tyler out.

"Somethin's not right here," Jonas said as soon as she'd closed the door behind her.

"I don't like it, either," Warren answered.

"Luther Vernon is on Dunlap's payroll. I don't trust him."

"We don't have anything to go on, Jonas."

Jonas scratched his chin, relieved that the child was safe, but feeling that he'd fallen short somehow and sensing they'd missed something. "Don't see how

Vernon could've searched in the dark. That ridge is mostly rock. Only a fool would ask his mount to do that."

"I'll ride out there and look around," Warren said.

"I'll go with you after I ride over to Doc's. Let's put somebody on the man's tail."

After Doc checked Tyler over and pronounced him unharmed, he gave Eliza a tin of salve. Lilibelle filled plates with food. Doc joined Ward in the dining room while Eliza sat with Tyler at the kitchen table.

The weary eight-year-old picked at his bacon and eggs. "My tummy feels kinda dizzy."

"Dr. McKee said you might feel that way, and possibly have a headache, too, from the bad-smelling stuff that put you to sleep. Have you thrown up?"

Tyler shook his head.

Daniel helped Ada heat water and fill the tub in the bathing chamber, then Daniel and Matt went off to school, Ward accompanying them out the front door.

Eliza led Tyler along the back hall to the bathing room and helped him undress and get into the water. After soaping his hair, she rinsed it. She had him stand so she could wash him and look him over. "Do you hurt anywhere else?" she asked.

He shook his head, but offered, "I lost my schoolbooks."

"I'm sure Miss Fletcher will replace them."

"Did Dan and Matt lose theirs, too?"

"I would guess so. Tyler, did anyone hurt you?"

"They wasn't very gentle, but they didn't hit me or nothin'. Why did somebody do that?"

"I don't know. But I was never more afraid in my whole life," she told him, drying his hair with a warm towel. "Do you think you can sleep now?"

"What about school?"

"You need to rest."

"But I already missed a day."

"If you feel up to it, you can go to school tomorrow."

She pulled the plug. He stepped out of the tub, and took the towel from her to dry himself. He stood wrapped in it while she dabbed salve on his sore wrists and wrapped strips of soft cotton fabric around them.

Once he was dressed and they had returned to their room, she pulled the curtains closed and tucked him into his narrow bed. "I'll sit here while you sleep," she assured him.

"Go work if you want, Aunt Liza," he told her, but his shaky voice wasn't very convincing. He was trying to act brave and grown-up.

She shook her head. "I don't want to leave you."

He closed his eyes, and she sat in the overstuffed chair nearby. Once she knew he was asleep, she moved to her bed and drifted off. She dreamed of her mother and Jenny Lee. They were eating tea cakes and talking on the sunny front porch. Jenny was laughing, her golden hair catching the sun, and Eliza kept filling the teapot and frosting more cakes. How many could they possibly hold?

A soft tapping woke her. She rose and padded forward. Expecting Jonas, she opened the door.

Phoebe stood in the hall. "Ward sent me. You have a visitor downstairs."

Groggy from the dream, she cleared her head. "Who is it?"

"Mr. Dunlap."

Royce had come here? She experienced a moment of panic.

"I'll come in and sit with Tyler," Phoebe told her.

Eliza glanced at her boy, still sleeping soundly. "All right. Thank you."

Downstairs, Royce waited in the foyer. "How are you faring, dear one?" he asked.

"I was resting."

"Forgive me for disturbing you," he said. "Is my son resting?"

"Tyler's sound asleep."

"We must speak. Is there somewhere private?"

Eliza glanced at Ward, and then led Royce around the front desk to the office. He entered behind her and closed the door.

She was fairly confident that he wouldn't make a scene with so many people nearby; still, she didn't want to listen to anything he had to say.

"Your days of behaving like a trollop are over," he announced in that pious tone.

She studied the oak woodwork for a long minute before looking at him. It gave her supreme satisfaction to see the cut at the corner of his mouth. He'd seen her reaction, and his nostrils flared. He tightened his lips, setting his thin mustache in a straight line. He'd changed into a clean white shirt. She refused to buy into his meanness by asking what he was talking about.

"You and the barkeep have been entirely too cozy, dear *sister*."

She remembered Willie's report of a rider following them out of town. "Are you following me?"

"I have better things to do with my time."

"I've often wondered what those things were."

"I have eyes and ears everywhere," he said. "And this latest tryst is finished, do you hear me? You're moving back to the house."

"I can't do that."

"Why not? If you're concerned about propriety, I'll hire you a companion until we're married. Someone proper, not a saloon girl."

"It's too difficult to be in that house now, since Jenny…" She let the words drift off.

"You're coming back. It might as well be sooner than later."

"I need more time."

"To do what? Get yourself up a stump by yet another miscreant? The next child will be my own son, I can assure you."

"What is the purpose, Royce?" she asked. "I'll give you my share of the company. That's all you've ever wanted. Jenny's share, then mine. If you have all that, why do you have to keep after me, as well? You don't love me. You never loved Jenny."

The room was too small. When he walked toward her, there was nowhere to go except backward into a wall. He took a strand of her hair and rubbed it between his fingers and thumb. "Power has nothing to do with love, foolish girl. I run the biggest company in this part of the state. People do what I tell them to do."

"Why isn't that enough?" she asked.

"I'll own Sutherland Brick Company lock, stock and barrel. But then it will be Dunlap Brick Company. And I'll have owned both Sutherland women. You'll be Dunlap property, too. I'll have everything your father once had and more."

Eliza swallowed.

"Jenny Lee wanted your bastard, not me. You'll do well to remember that. Taking him made Jenny Lee happy and pacified your father. Pretending that I cared made me look good. Henry's not watching anymore."

"Tyler's a Dunlap in the eyes of Silver Bend."

"Not as far as I'm concerned. I want my own son."

Even if she was planning to stay and keep Tyler here, he wouldn't acknowledge him as a son? The more she heard, the more certain she was that leaving was the right thing—the *only* thing to do. She was done begging and pleading with a man who had no conscience. "What do you want from me?"

"You're going to move back to the house. Then you're going to marry me and be a good little wife."

"And the alternative?"

"Your precious boy will be all yours, which suits you in one respect. On the other hand, everyone will know you're a whore and that he's a bastard."

He backed away, his smug expression showing how

pleased he was with himself. "I'll be mortified that the news leaked out, of course. I had tried so hard to protect you and your son and give the boy a good name."

"Give me two weeks to find a companion. I may have to advertise out of town."

"One week. At that time I will let it be known that we are observing a mourning period and then we will marry. For the boy's sake, of course. And to keep the family legacy intact."

"Of course."

"And no more dallying with the barkeeper."

"You don't know what you're talking about."

"Stay clear of him. If you don't take me seriously, see what happens."

"What more could happen?"

"Oh?" He walked to the door and rested his hand on the knob. "He could get shot. Again."

Royce opened the door and let himself out.

Eliza stared at the back of the oak door. Shot again. Meaning he would shoot him or have him shot? Again, meaning he had something to do with the last time?

She raised her hand to her breast as the implication and the threat swirled in her mind and settled into cohesive assumptions.

If he was having her followed, then he knew where she went and who she went with. He couldn't see inside these walls, but someone could have observed them on the porch that night and shot at Jonas.

Why? To get him out of the picture?

She had never doubted Royce's determination or the heights he would scale in order to get what he wanted. He was devious enough to paint himself in a flattering light while working his selfish strategy behind the scenes.

She had no doubt he would stop at nothing to carry out his plan, but as more and more facts came to light, it had become clear that the situation was perilous. Everything that mattered was at stake. Her freedom, Tyler's future, their safety….

Everything.

Chapter Sixteen

Eliza Jane remained in her room most of the day and throughout the evening. Nadine had carried up food for her and Tyler. When Jonas stopped by to check on them, Eliza Jane seemed reluctant to talk and eager to be left alone.

They'd been through a terrible ordeal, he understood, so he respected her privacy and worked late. With the niggling question of Luther Vernon's ease in locating Tyler, he strolled down the street and settled at a table in the saloon.

Luther was playing cards with a handful of the regulars, and from the looks of it, the stakes were pretty high. He pulled a fistful of cigars from his vest pocket and passed them out. The men scraped matches over the edge of the table and lit up. A pungent cloud formed over the table and hung in the air.

Quay brought Jonas a glass of beer with a yeasty head of foam and set it down.

"How long's this been goin' on," Jonas asked.

"Since this afternoon. He's throwing around that reward money and buyin' rounds for the house."

"Peaceful enough?" Jonas asked.

"No problems." Quay spoke in a low tone. "Luther's been in Silver Bend maybe two or three years now, would you say? I've never seen him with money before, and I guess now I know why."

Jonas nodded, visiting with a few men, until the hour grew late. He helped close up and tip chairs upside down on the tables. Eventually, he headed home to his quarters, washed and settled in to read. The journals had become his regular pastime, a link to the father he'd never really known. Through them, his father had transformed from a shadowy absent figure to a man sick with regret and grief, a man doing the best he could.

Still not sleepy, Jonas put the last journal back in the trunk, pausing over the packets of his parents' letters. Resigned to reading through them, he settled comfortably in his chair. The missives from his father were reserved accounts of his days and the work he was doing. He spoke more passionately of the battles, the principles and beliefs behind them, and often mentioned his desire to make a difference.

He'd written in a letter stamped with one of the later postmarks:

I miss you and our son more than words can say. Jonas is a bright boy with a stubborn streak that will carry him far, as well as back him into corners, depending on how wisely he chooses.

When I return this time, I plan to stay home for good. It's been difficult for you, alone during these months that have turned to years, and my growing desire is to spend the rest of my days and nights with you, my dear wife.

I have deliberated on a project that Jonas and I can work on together and have chosen one to complete first. We will dig that root cellar you have always wanted and plant a garden. You can pickle beets for him to turn up his nose at.

Jonas detested pickled beets. His father had known that?

Every letter was signed, "with unflagging love for you and our son." As a boy growing up without a father present, he'd believed that his father had simply cared more for his travels and his work than for his wife and family. A world of hurt had partnered with those beliefs. He'd learned respect for women by seeing his mother's strength, but he admired her all the more now, recognizing how much she had sacrificed to help the man she loved follow his heart and live by his principles.

Jonas had never set out to become a hero. Defending those weaker than him was something that came over him as instinctively as raising his fists to a bully. Didn't take a genius to recognize he'd harbored guilt and regret over being unable to protect his mother or that he hadn't been able to set it aside.

For years he'd resented his father for not being there when she'd needed him most. Helping people was Jonas's way of making up for his weakness back then. It was his way of being unlike his father.

But his father had been helping people, too. He'd slept in tents and traveled with the army because he believed in what he was doing. A new understanding of the man and his work took some shifting of notions in Jonas's stubborn head. He'd always seen his father's profession as abandonment and—more importantly— as the reason for his mother's death.

His father's commitment to the army and the men who served, was an extension of his compassion for people. His written regrets melted through the cold resentment in Jonas's heart. He should have forgiven the man long ago.

It was time to let go of the resentment. But he couldn't pick up regret, either. That's what his father had done and it had destroyed him. Jonas had come back to Silver Bend. He'd spent time with his father before his death. He'd done the best he could at the time.

That knowledge would have to be good enough.

That night Eliza dreamed of the sunroom at the house. She and Jenny sat on a flowered sofa faded by years of sunlight and watched Tyler playing on one of the quilts their mother had sewn. The pale-haired infant entertained himself with a stack of painted blocks and his wooden horses.

"He's the best thing that ever happened to me," Jenny

Lee told her. Her blue eyes reflected love and her fair hair glistened in the sunlight. "You know that, don't you?"

Eliza had nodded.

"Will you always remember how very happy I am right this moment? Years from now, when you question yourself or think back, will you remember? Please say yes."

"Yes," Eliza had told her. "I'll remember."

Eliza woke with tears on her temples and homesick disappointment lying heavily on her heart. "I remember," she whispered into the darkness.

Jonas and Eliza walked Tyler and the Harper boys all the way to school the following morning. She wanted to bend down and wrap her arms around her child, but he gave them a goodbye wave and headed for the little brick building.

Eliza watched with her heart in her throat.

Partway there, his steps slowed. He turned back to face them. In the next instant, he was running toward Eliza full tilt. He threw his arms around her waist and hugged her with all the strength in his scrawny little arms. The Harpers grinned and waited.

"I'm gonna be fine," he told her, leaning back to look up at her.

She knelt. "I know you will."

"Don't worry about me, 'kay?"

"Okay," she said, but the word was spoken around tears. She stood.

Matt and Daniel followed him inside.

"Maybe someone should be here to watch over the school today," she suggested.

"Warren has somebody on that," Jonas replied. "He deputized Earl Mobley's nephew. Uriah will be checkin' on them through the day and meetin' 'em after school."

With that assurance, she felt marginally better about Tyler's safety. Adding what had happened to the uppermost burden on her mind, she still had plenty to worry about. Royce's threat that she stay away from Jonas was alarming.

They headed back along Main Street, the brims of their hats shading their eyes from the bright morning sun. She couldn't help checking the doorways and windows above the street. Jonas had always made her feel secure. Knowing him…*loving him*…had been a balm to her lonely, aching heart. And without a doubt, she did love him. That was why she had to protect him as fiercely as she protected Tyler. Someone could be watching them right now, ready to put a bullet in his heart.

Royce had as much as admitted he was responsible for Jonas being shot. He wasn't going to stop now. He wouldn't stop until he had what he wanted. To calm the rapid increase of her heartbeat, she took a deep breath. "I'll be moving back to the house next week."

She waited for his reaction.

His face didn't reveal his thoughts, but he asked, "So soon?"

"I have to go back eventually. And you don't really

need me to do the books any longer. Your arm is much better."

"I thought you were avoidin' bein' improper and all that."

"I'll be hiring a companion." What was she doing? Lying to him as well as to Royce? It would be too unfair to go through the motions and hire someone and then disappear.

And there was no point in moving to the house, because once she had no income, there was no reason to stay. She hadn't earned nearly enough money. Royce kept cutting her time shorter and shorter.

Royce had most likely hired someone to shoot Jonas. The fact that Jonas wasn't already dead was no thanks to a lack of effort. As easily as that shot had come out of nowhere in the night, it could happen again.

After her dream last night, she hadn't been able to return to sleep. She'd lain in bed, later stared out the window into the darkness, then sat in the chair and listened to Tyler's breathing. And all the while she'd been thinking. Racking her brain for a better solution.

The confusion and constant fear created by the whole situation nauseated her. It took all her strength of will not to cry, not to pour out the truth. But she didn't want to handle the consequences.

There were only two choices.

Staying and buckling under to Royce's demands, becoming his wife was an alternative she couldn't accept. Maybe it was selfish, but she couldn't do it. Where would he stop? As long as she lived, he would have ammunition to hold over her head—and over Tyler's, as well. Even if she protected Tyler for as long as she could, Royce might still ruin his life once he was a grown man.

The other option was to disappear. And it was still the best choice. It wasn't only her welfare she was looking out for, so it wasn't entirely selfish. But she wouldn't get a hundred miles without sufficient money.

There was one thing she owned that would give her the capital she so badly needed.

She'd never gone back to sleep after that nostalgic dream. She'd sat in the darkness, wishing for a time and place like she'd once known. A time of innocence and freedom. A place of security and acceptance.

In all the thinking, she'd decided what she must do to survive.

"I have a proposition for you."

He pushed the brim of his hat back with a thumb and paused on the boardwalk to look at her.

She stopped beside him.

"Gonna forget the paperwork this mornin'?" The twinkle in his eyes told her he had something entirely different in mind.

Her heart fluttered at the thought, but she pushed it aside. "A business proposition," she clarified.

"Oh." He shrugged. "What is it?"

"I'd like you to buy my share of the brickyard."

"What?"

"I've seen the numbers you move around and I've tallied your deposits. If you can't pay the entire amount, you could borrow the rest. I assure you I'll give you a good deal."

"What're you thinkin'?" he asked, putting a hand at his hip, his elbow cocked out. "Your share guarantees you an income for life. Or as long as the company is sound, and I don't see that changin'."

"Only if I remain single. If I marry, whatever was mine becomes my husband's."

He frowned first, then his expression immediately changed to one of discomfort. "Don't know what t' say. You won't let me talk about that. I'd marry you tomorrow if—"

"I know." She raised her hand to silence him.

"There you go. Stiflin' me when I go t'say it. What in tarnation do you want of me, Eliza Jane?"

"I want you to buy my share of Sutherland Brick."

"If you married me, and the share legally became mine on paper, or if I paid you for it, what would be the difference? Except I wouldn't want your shares. I don't know the first thing about manufacturin' bricks. I have my own properties and investments."

Well, she'd stuck her foot in it now. She'd crossed into an area she'd never wanted to discuss. "The difference is I'd have the money."

"Well, there's where your thinkin' is clear as mud. Then the money would become mine instead of the shares. Legally speakin' is all."

Frustrated, Eliza planted her feet and looked him in the eye. "We're not marrying, you and I, so that won't happen."

"But you said you wanted to sell your share so it didn't become your husband's." It was plain that he was aggravated enough to bite nails. He narrowed his gaze. "Are you talkin' about marrying' someone *else?*"

"I'm not talking about anyone, no."

His frustration had been replaced by a flash of hurt, but immediately he masked his feelings with a tight-lipped glower. "So, what has all this been, Eliza Jane? You and me. What am I to you? Someone to ease your grief and help pass the time till you're ready to move on?"

"Here isn't the place to discuss this," she told him, glancing for the first time at the nearby windows of the bank and at the hardware store across the street where Yale came out with a broom.

"Morning, Miss Sutherland. I trust your nephew is fine."

"Yes, thank you. He went to school."

"Let's go talk in private then," Jonas said from beside her.

"I don't think that's a good idea."

"Why not? Runnin' out of excuses? Or your interest in me just suddenly tumbled?"

"It's not like that."

He surged forward along the boardwalk, his boot heels hitting the wood in rapid succession. Eliza had to half run to catch up to him. "Jonas, wait!"

He reached the door and held it open, stepping aside and waiting for her to enter the hotel. "You can report to Ada this mornin'," he said. "You're right about my arm. I can handle the ledgers."

She tried not to be hurt that he'd dismissed her from his presence. She'd been evasive and downright mean with her lack of explanations and deserved his ire. He had every right to be angry. She'd never wanted to hurt him, but she had. And still he remained her best hope. "Will you think about buying my share?"

"I'll ponder it."

She nodded. "Thank you."

Jonas watched her climb the stairs, a hard knot of confusion in his belly. As mad as he was, he could still see past it to recognize that something was wrong. Here she was seeking money. Again. This time an exorbitant amount.

He could come up with it, he figured. He didn't know the exact figures involved, but he'd inherited his father's savings, was drawing interest from a big percent of his army pay, and had profits coming in from three flourishing businesses.

But why did she want to sell so badly? What did she need money for? Why had she wanted to work in the first place?

Heading back to the office, his thoughts straggled back to the conclusion he'd come to before: she was planning to run away. He'd glossed over that assumption, but he'd been fooling himself. The theory was believable. She needed money. She didn't plan to be here come fall. And she had never planned for their relationship to be permanent.

He still didn't know who Tyler's father was. If it was Dunlap, Jonas couldn't stand by and let her take his boy and run. Just being a jerk wasn't a reason to lose your kid for life, but the way she behaved around Dunlap made it pretty clear he was holding something over her head.

It was his nature to think over all the aspects. The boy deserved a father, but he needed a father that showed him some love. Royce had never even shown the slightest interest.

And Jonas wasn't convinced Dunlap was Tyler's father, and if he was, that he hadn't forced himself on her. In that case, he didn't have any rights.

Jonas had to make some decisions.

It ate at him all day, her refusal to let him in on what was going on. That night he again observed Luther spending money in the saloon. Long about ten, his cash ran out.

"Think he went through five hundred dollars?" Jonas asked Quay.

"Pert near," the man replied. "He has new duds, and this afternoon he brung gifts for the girls. Scarves and such. Mrs. Holmes and Rowena left theirs on the bar."

Luther's popularity waned with his spending money, and by eleven, he grabbed his hat and left the saloon.

Jonas walked out behind him and watched him untether his mount and ride off. From the doorway, Jonas gave Quay a nod and turned to head home. A relaxing bath sounded good, so he heated water and filled a tub, sinking into the steaming depths and closing his eyes.

Part of him wished Eliza Jane would come looking

for him tonight. Part of him wished he'd never lost his good sense and gotten involved. He didn't know how much longer he could stand by. Maybe he'd been too patient.

He'd never be in this room again without thinking of her, without remembering their steamy lovemaking and her ivory beauty in the gaslight. The more he thought about it—about her—the more he fumed.

Enough of her evasion; he was full up to his gullet with that foolishness. Restraining himself was the hardest thing he'd ever done. He'd jumped into scuffles with men three times the size of that curvy temptress, raised both fists and come out unscathed. Why was he holding back? He had no reason to worry about scaring her off now. She was planning to go anyhow.

Releasing the water down the drain, he rose from the tub, dried and dressed, tucking in his shirttail haphazardly. Grabbing up his hat, holster and boots, he dropped them off in his rooms on his way up to the third floor.

Chapter Seventeen

Eliza was sitting in the chair near the table and lamp, unable to concentrate on the book in her hands. At the firm rap on the door, she jumped, the book falling to the floor with a thud.

Tyler didn't move.

She got up and padded to the door. "Who is it?" she asked, barely above a whisper.

"Me."

Her heart jumped again. She opened the door and slipped out into the hall, pulling the door closed behind her. Jonas's dark hair was wet and standing in disarray. The clean enticing scents of soap and man assaulted her senses. "Did you make a decision?"

"Nadine is gonna stay with Tyler while you and I go over a few things."

She hadn't noticed the slender young woman standing a few feet away in the hall. Her skirt and twisted shirtwaist looked as though she'd yanked them on in a hurry. Eliza gave her a feeble smile. "What are you doing?" she whispered to Jonas.

"We're gonna talk."

Not will you talk to me, not please let's talk, but we're going to. His bullheadedness had Eliza's hackles up. She'd had enough of men telling her what to do. "We've pretty much said it all unless you have an answer about the shares."

"Not all," he disagreed. "You haven't said anything that made sense yet," he told her. "C'mon now, before we make a scene in the hall."

She hadn't changed into her nightclothes yet, so it wasn't that him calling on her was such an inconvenience. She looked at Nadine again. "Thank you. I'm sorry you got dragged out of your bed."

"It's all right. I wasn't asleep yet." She raised a book that she'd been holding at her side. "I can read here just as well as in my room."

"Lock the door behind us," Eliza told her and watched the young woman go into the room. The key turned in the lock.

Jonas gestured toward the stairs. She marched up ahead of him.

"This was uncalled for," she told him as he opened the door to his quarters and stood back to let her pass.

He locked the door and dropped the key into the pocket of his trousers. The air in the room seemed too close, and she fought back a rising edge of panic. He meant her no harm, she was sure of that. But his demanding behavior could make trouble for her.

"What's uncalled for," he answered, "is the way you've avoided comin' right out and tellin' me what's goin' on." He gestured to a side table. "Like somethin' to drink? Sherry maybe?"

"This isn't a social visit. Or a seduction," she answered. "You ordered me out of my bed as though you have the right."

"Some things need discussin'," he told her. "Like the reason you're hell bent to get your hands on cash."

"It's actually none of your business," she said, bristling.

"I think different. First the job, now the shares. A body would think you're aimin' to take off with that money and not be seen again."

Eliza felt heated color rise in her cheeks at his clever suspicions. He was backing her up against a wall, and she had no choice left but to flee or fight. "And what if I was? It would still be none of your business. You don't have any holds on me."

He gestured to the divan. "Have a seat."

"No."

He sat on an upholstered chair and sighed. "Eliza Jane, I know some things that I haven't let on about."

A buzz filled her ears, and fear made her frame tremble. "Like what?"

"I know Tyler is your boy. That you gave birth to him, not your sister."

Her knees shook so hard and her head felt so light, she swayed on her feet.

Jonas jumped up and took her arm to guide her to the

divan. He poured her a glass of water and offered it to her as though a drink was the solution to her life.

But she accepted it with cold trembling fingers and drank half of it before handing it back. He set down the tumbler and resumed his seat. Waiting.

"What—how—" she stammered.

"Have a trunk full of my father's journals. He kept records of all his calls on the local folks. Right detailed accounts. On Tyler's date of birth, he helped bring Tyler into the world. And into your arms. Not Jenny Lee's. She was too weak-hearted to carry and birth a baby. You were strong and healthy."

Eliza sat in shocked silence until eventually her ears stopped humming and her shaking subsided. After what seemed a lifetime of resolving herself, she met his eyes with shame. "My father insisted I give Jenny my baby."

Hard as she tried to keep emotion from her voice and her heart, all the pain and rejection sprang to life as fresh as the day she'd handed her child into her sister's arms. "He was so angry with me. So disappointed. And I was a woman with a child out of wedlock. I didn't have options."

"Wondered how you hid your condition from the town."

"I stayed home with Jenny the last few months. When Nora came over, we filled out Jenny's nightdress with a pillow and I stayed in my room. We simply told people Jenny needed bed rest throughout the trying ordeal, and that I was taking care of her."

Jonas nodded his understanding. He looked contemplative before he said, "How does Royce fit into all this?"

Just her brother-in-law's name made Eliza's stomach dip with nausea. "He placated my father in every regard. He wanted esteem and position, and if making Jenny happy made my father happy, he was willing to go along with it."

"I'm still perplexed," Jonas said. "What part did he play in Tyler's comin' into the world? Did he rape you? Did you sleep with him willin'ly?"

Eliza looked up, stunned that he had suspected something like that. "No! No, he's not Tyler's father."

Jonas's shoulders relaxed a slight measure. "Glad for that. I would have had to stop you for certain if I thought you were runnin' off with his son." But he frowned and looked at her with that leveled stare that went right into her soul. "The man you told me about then?"

She nodded. "I was a foolish girl. I believed Forest loved me and that he had honorable intentions. He was my father's bright young protégé, and when I told him about the baby, he said we'd tell my father and be married. I believed him." She smoothed her skirt, reliving the painful happenings. "We were going to tell him the following day. Forest would come to dinner as he often did, and afterward he would approach Father in his study.

"He never showed up that night." Her voice lowered with the telling. "I made an excuse for him, then went the following day, hoping to find him at the factory. My father said he'd left, packed his things and gone. He couldn't figure out his sudden departure.

"I was stunned, of course. But I couldn't tell my father about the baby or the plans we'd made. I waited, praying it was a mistake or a cruel joke and that he'd be back and everything would be fine. But then I started getting sick…and…well, finally Jenny guessed."

"Sorry the scoundrel hurt you," Jonas told her in a gravelly voice.

His sympathy brought her back on track. "Eventually, I had to tell Father, of course. He was furious. Called me terrible names. Accused me of running off his favorite choice for someone to take over once he was too advanced in years. Of course I had always dreamed that person would be me, but I was never good enough in his eyes."

The memories remained fresh and painful. "He was so angry," she went on. "He banished me from the brickyard and warned me that if I played the harlot with any more of his employees, he'd send me away. A few days later, we were all seated at the dinner table. He announced that I would be giving the baby to Jenny Lee and Royce, and that the child would be theirs from that moment on.

"Jenny Lee was beside herself with joy, of course. She thought he'd spoken to me privately and that we'd come to the decision together." Eliza remembered vividly the contrast between her sister's happiness and her misery. For Jenny's sake, she'd hidden her pain, but at a deep cost.

"Royce wore a smug expression because he'd already stepped into Forest's shoes as father's right-hand man. He patted Jenny's hand and told her the baby would always be theirs and how he'd be so proud to be working to make a place for a future heir in the company."

"Then why all the running and fear I see in your eyes?" Jonas asked.

"He waited for Jenny to die. Like a vulture circling over her bed. It made me sick. Now if I don't agree to marry him, he will tell the truth about Tyler. I can't let that happen. I can't ruin Tyler's life like that."

"And you can't call Dunlap's bluff?"

"How? Risk Tyler finding out he's illegitimate and being called names until he's forced to leave town?"

Jonas pressed the knuckle of his thumb against his teeth in a thinking pose.

"Guess that's not gonna work." He studied her expression and her hands clenched in her lap. "Why didn't you trust me enough to just tell me?"

"I didn't want you to think badly of me like my father did. Like Royce does."

"If he thinks so poorly of you, then why…? Oh. He wants your share of the company once you're married."

She nodded. "That's it. He doesn't really care about me. Or about Tyler. We're just possessions to him."

Jonas got up and came to perch beside her on the divan, where he took her hands in his and warmed them. "I could never think poorly of you. Don't you know that? You loved Forest, and you trusted him. After that

I'm surprised you even trusted me enough to… You don't trust me, do you?"

"You're an honorable man," she told him. "You care deeply about people and about doing the right thing. I guess it was my heart I didn't want to risk again. But it's too late for that."

He tightened his grasp on her hands. "What do you mean?"

"I mean I fell in love with you. But you must know that. If I didn't love you…"

"Wouldn't have made love with me. Never thought you were foolin' with my affections. Just figured you were confused maybe. And I knew you'd been hurt." He put his arm around her and pulled her close. "I love you, too, but you'd never let me say it."

She placed her hand against his chest, felt the steady beat of his heart and wished love was enough. Her eyes filled with tears. She closed them and raised her lips for a kiss.

He obliged her, tucking his hand alongside her cheek and angling his face over hers in a warm exchange filled with as much emotion as she'd ever felt from him. If only his love…his kiss…was enough to banish the demons that were her reality.

He kissed her nose and her eyelids, holding her…his loving embrace was what dreams were made of.

"This doesn't change anything," she whispered. She wanted to cry, but held back a torrent of tears. "Nothing is going to stop Royce. I still have two choices left. Marry him or run."

"I'll confront him," he declared.

"You can't, don't you see? If you oppose him, if he doesn't get his way, he'll expose my secret. I can't allow that to happen to Tyler. I can't. Not at the expense of Tyler's happiness."

"Then I'll come with you. We'll leave together and make a family somewhere far away from here."

Eliza edged away and stared at him in disbelief. "Jonas! You have a life here. You've worked hard to have this."

"So have you."

"But I have no choice. You do."

"And I'd choose to leave so we could be together. I could start over again."

"I could never ask that of you."

"You didn't."

She shook her head, sadness filling her until nothing was left. No hope, no promises.

He pressed his mouth into a line. "That's it, I reckon. You *didn't* ask it of me, did you?"

"Not for the reason you're thinking," she was quick to assure him. "Not because I don't love you or want you. But because it's no way to build a life. Not running. Changing our names might not even work. We might have a chance if it's just Tyler and I, but the three of us?

"He'd never stop looking if he thought I had run off with you, Jonas. He would never stop chasing you if he thought you took something that belonged to him."

"I'm not afraid of him."

"But I am. And for good reason."

His eyes held the same bleakness she felt inside. He'd just offered to dump his whole life for her and she'd said no thanks.

He released her, moving to stand beside the cold fireplace and stare at the ticking clock on the mantel. "I'll buy your shares. Say how much. You want it transferred somewhere?"

"Royce would find out."

"Cash then."

"Yes."

"When?"

"I can hold him off a few more days while I go through the motions of hiring a companion."

"Ask Maddie or Nadine to stay with you if you want."

"You mean…?"

"Tell one of 'em you'd like their company as a favor for a few days or a week or as long as you like, and that I'll still pay their wages here."

"I couldn't do that."

"Why not?" He turned his gaze on her. "You don't want my help?"

"I don't want to take advantage of you." She balled her fists in her lap. "I regret how unhappy I've made you."

"Think on what will happen after you're gone and Dunlap finds out I'm his new partner. That should cheer you up."

"I'll be leaving you with a steaming kettle of fish, won't I?" It wasn't as if she didn't have her own worries.

What would she tell Tyler? How would she support them? She could barely hear herself think for all the unanswered questions screeching in her head.

He took a breath and stretched his sore arm and shoulder, but he didn't reply. "Will I hear from you? After you're gone?"

"I don't know. Do you think it would be safe for me to write? I don't want him coming after me."

"Reckon you'll have to do what you need to. It's just… Well, I'll be here if you need me."

Eliza's heart couldn't bear any more grief. Aside from giving away her baby, telling Jonas the truth had been the most difficult thing she'd ever done up to this point. But now she had to leave, with both of them knowing it was forever. This would be the end.

It took all her courage to focus on the outcome she needed and not on what she wanted. "We'll work out the money tomorrow then," she said.

He nodded his agreement.

Feeling empty inside, she stood and walked toward the door. A moment later, she was standing in the hall. Bereft.

She was closer to her goal than she'd ever been; she had to remember that. It had been foolish to allow confusion and add to the problem by involving Jonas…by falling in love with him. It was cruel of her to hurt him.

She had to change her focus or she would break down and never get control of her emotions again. She had plenty else to think about, so she averted her thoughts and emotions. She'd said nothing to Tyler about their leaving. How was she going to pack, get him on a train and out of town without him inquiring about Royce or where they were going? She'd wait until the last minute.

Someone else, perhaps Ward, could take their belongings to the station. She would have to check departure times. When Tyler got up and dressed, she could divert him to the station and tell him they were going to have an adventure.

She would ask Ada or Maddie to check the train schedules and purchase tickets for her. Eliza supposed it was time she thought about where they were going. Once they'd arrived at their first destination, they would change names and head out again. It was the best plan she had.

And she had to keep herself moving forward from here on out.

The following morning, Eliza was carrying a stack of clean sheets across the upstairs landing that looked down on the lobby when she saw Luther enter and speak to Ward at the desk. Ward said something to him, and Luther left.

Ward found her making a bed. "Letter for you, Miss Sutherland."

He hurried away, and she broke the wax seal and unfolded the parchment.

I've made an appointment at the jeweler's this afternoon. Meet me precisely at two o'clock.

The jeweler's? No doubt now Royce was planning to purchase or order a wedding ring. As soon as that happened, rumors would spread. She'd be trapped into more lies and evasions.

More orders. More demands. But not for long.

She stewed until time grew near for her to go face him, then washed up, changed her clothing and repinned her hair.

"I have an appointment," she told Ada. "I should be back in time to go walk the boys home."

She didn't have far to go. The only jeweler was a watchmaker who kept a storefront on Oak Boulevard, just around the corner and north of Main Street. On the corner opposite her, in front of the hardware store, Luther Vernon lounged against one of the pillars that held up the wooden awnings above the boardwalk across the street. He watched her from beneath the brim of his hat, a lit cheroot between his teeth.

After her initial surprise, Eliza looked away and continued her journey. He was watching her, no doubt about it. He'd probably been watching her less blatantly for a long time.

She turned the corner and continued toward the watchmaker's. Royce's buggy was already sitting in the street, a glossy black horse hitched to it. The Sutherland's previous buggy had been adequate, but he'd ordered this one a year ago and had it shipped from Pittsburgh.

Eliza steeled herself as she neared the building and opened the weathered door. A bell rang above her head.

The interior smelled of oil and aged wood, and the floorboards creaked as she moved into the room.

"Good afternoon, my dear," Royce said, coming to take her hand and press his lips against the backs of her fingers. She wanted to yank it away, but she endured the greeting and met Mr. Atwell's curious bespectacled gaze. She only knew him by profession, since she'd never been in his shop before. She offered him a stilted smile.

Royce gestured to a wooden chair. "Have a seat. Mr. Atwell will bring a few rings to gauge sizes and a catalog for you to look at."

Eliza took the offered seat, smoothing her skirts nervously. She guessed it shouldn't matter what Royce did with the money she was leaving behind. Her father's money. Her and Jenny's inheritance. If she got a ring before she left, she could always sell it. Her attention wavered to the largest diamond on the display board Mr. Atwell brought to her. She didn't know much about diamonds, but it looked like a large one, and eight small rubies surrounded the stone in a gaudy setting that made the ring look like a flower with a giant center.

"I don't keep many on hand," he told her. "But I can order anything you like from New York."

"Actually," Eliza said, raising a slender finger to point. "I rather like that one."

The older man's expression brightened and he smiled. "The lady has excellent taste. This diamond is first quality. One and three-quarters carat, actually. Plus Burmese rubies."

He took it from the tray and handed it to her.

Eliza slid the ring on the appropriate finger. Odd that Royce was going through this farce after stealing her and Jenny's jewelry. Of course this was a display of ownership. Part of his ruthless desire to possess Sutherland property. Perhaps the money from her mother's jewels would pay for this ring.

"You can choose another from the catalog if you'd prefer something less ostentatious," Royce told her.

"No, I quite like this one," she told him with a smile. Someone as obsessed with material things as Royce would appreciate a mercenary motive. "In fact, I can't imagine liking one more."

Chapter Eighteen

Royce gave the shop owner a peeved glance.

Eliza pretended to admire the jewels on her hand, holding the ring up to allow the light to reflect the facets. "I'll be the envy of all the other wives."

Immediately, Royce recovered his display of generous affection. "Of course, my love. Only the best for you. Does it fit? Mr. Atwell can correct the size."

Truth was, the fit was a tad snug, but she wasn't about to let this asset out of her sight or off her finger.

"It was made for me," she replied, gazing at the jewel-encrusted ring on her hand as though it held some profound meaning.

"Our engagement is official." Royce took her hand and looked into her eyes. To anyone else the gesture would appear romantic. Eliza understood the intent. "You won't remove it."

"No. I won't take it off."

"I'll purchase an announcement in the *Sentinel* to run next week."

Did he think he was scaring her? "I'll order invitations." She opened her eyes wide as though concerned. "We haven't set a date yet."

"Would you like to pay for the ring now, or start an account?" Mr. Atwell interrupted.

Royce turned a harsh look on him. "I'll send my man to pay for it this afternoon."

The shop owner nodded. "Very well. You're a trustworthy fellow."

Eliza stood and took the arm that Royce offered. He led her out of doors, where she raised her hand for the sunlight to catch the diamond.

"I'm not fooled," Royce stated.

Her heart skittered, but she kept her smile serene. "Whatever are you talking about?"

"I don't believe for a moment that you've suddenly become a submissive and tolerant fiancée." He gestured to the buggy and took her elbow.

"You haven't given me any choices, but to make the best of my situation." She allowed him to assist her and seated herself.

He came around and climbed up, taking the reins and setting the horse in motion.

"If I'm to be your wife," she said, "I'm going to be your wife in style." She'd caught the spirit of the charade. "Why be glum and feel sorry for myself when I can enjoy the privileges of being the wife of the richest man in Silver Bend? Why, I might have to start a new ladies' society."

Of course this one wouldn't be women who'd seen Jonas Black naked. "How do you like the Society of Businessmen's Wives? That will make people take notice."

A blank look encompassed his face for a second, but apparently the thought of a society wife held enough appeal to delude him into thinking she could endure their marriage for the sake of money and position. An uncertain, but smug smile turned his mustache upward on the side she could see. He turned toward her, and she noticed his overlapping tooth, but instead met his eyes.

He could relate to someone as ruthless and driven as he, so she would work a different perspective to keep him unsuspecting. She hoped her smile appeared as cold-blooded as his.

"I am interviewing women tomorrow," she told him. "As soon as I've selected someone, I'll have my things moved home. And after we're married, she'll be staying on as my personal companion."

"Maid?" he asked.

"Yes, of course, but that has such an intolerant air. I shall call her my companion."

"See that it's someone who will care for the boy, as well."

"You know I want to look after Tyler myself," she said in the insistent manner he would believe. "But it would be nice to have help when I want to go out or entertain."

Luther was no longer on the corner of Main and

Oak, though she looked along the street both ways to see if he was somewhere else spying.

"This is going to be an arrangement we can both live with," he told her. "Fortunately for your sake—and the barkeep's—you've come to your senses."

"I'd prefer we didn't discuss what's taken place in the past," she told him. "If this is going to be a suitable partnership, we have to start over."

"Hopefully, there will be no need for me to remind you of the past," he told her, his warning as poignant as ever.

She cast him a disdainful look, but remained what must seem to him obediently quiet.

"What will you tell anyone who inquires about the ring, since you're not inclined to remove it?" he asked as they neared the hotel.

She gave him a sideways glance. "Why, the truth, of course." After a moment of silence, she added, "That we have plans to marry, but we're waiting to announce our engagement publicly."

He reined the horse to a stop before the wide doorway and grabbed her arm.

"I don't know what your new game is, but just remember this. Whatever it is, if you make me look bad or try to play me for a fool, you'll pay for it."

He always had to have the last word. She jerked her arm away. Before he could make a move to get down, she jumped from the buggy to the street on her own. She turned to look up at him. "I'll let you know when I make a selection."

With that, she turned and left him sitting with a startled look on his normally arrogant face. Once inside, she darted to the shuttered front window, and through the wooden slats watched the black buggy pull away.

"Everything all right?"

At Jonas's voice, she spun to face him, holding her left hand down at her side. "Everything's fine." A quick glance told her Ward was watching, too. She checked her brooch with her right hand. "I'll be running along to fetch the boys soon."

"Want company?"

She thought of Luther loitering in wait for her. She didn't need news about her keeping company with Jonas to get back to Royce. "We'll do fine, thanks. Uriah will probably be watching the school from his post across the street at the jail."

Jonas nodded and grabbed his hat from behind the front desk, settling it on his head. He'd most likely seen her return with Royce, but he said nothing and left, heading toward the Silver Star.

She twisted the ring inward so that the jewels were on the bottom side. After dealing with her brother-in-law, Eliza felt in need of a bath and a good scrubbing. She tried to shake off the feeling. She might have confused Royce today, but she had no illusions that he was any less dangerous.

She intended to take great care with everything she did from here on out.

Nadine was delighted to accompany Eliza for a few days. Eliza briefly considered taking the woman into her confidence; after all, many of the girls here had escaped brutal men and all would understand. Not doing so wasn't because she didn't trust her. Eliza simply couldn't bring herself to share her story or to place even the tiniest bit of risk on her and Tyler escaping without mishap.

"Have you ever met my brother-in-law, Royce Dunlap?"

"Don't believe so."

"So he wouldn't recognize you if he saw you."

"I don't see how."

When Eliza told Nadine that they were going to pretend to hire her as a companion, the girl didn't blink an eye. "We're going to tell him you've recently arrived from Boston. He wants me to have a companion, and I'm going to stall him for the time being."

Nadine laughed. "I can affect a Boston accent, listen to this." And she proceeded to recite a bawdy poem in a delightfully stilted inflection.

Eliza giggled and raised her hands to her cheeks. "However did you learn that?"

"My life before Montana was pretty much a series of cons. A beast of a man put me up to them and took every nickel I made. Finally I ran from him and made it as far as Cheyenne before I ran out of money and food and was ready to do something worse to survive—not that I'm passing judgment on anyone who's had to do that, mind you—when Jonas found me sleeping in a stable."

"In Wyoming?"

Nadine nodded. "Talk about fortune smiling on me

that night. He could have been anyone." She shook her head slightly as though she still couldn't believe her good fortune. "Jonas was traveling through. He asked where I was going, and I made up some outrageous lie. When he offered to let me ride with him, I suspected he had an ulterior motive, but I was too tired and hungry to care, so I went along.

"We camped along the trail, and he never laid a finger on me. Never even suggested it. He bought a couple of horses, and I rode alone then. Once we got to Silver Bend he offered me a job. I thought I knew what kind of job, but he assured me it would be a respectable position, and he'd count on me to keep it that way. He's the best man I've ever known."

Eliza understood better than most the passion behind Jonas's need to protect those who needed help. He'd been so young when his mother had been killed. He must have felt helpless. He could easily have learned to see the world as a cruel unjust place, and maybe he did, but he also stood up to do something about it.

That was only one of the many reasons she loved him. "He's the best man I've ever known, as well," Eliza told her.

Eliza had experienced an abundance of loss in her life. Leaving him was going to be yet another level of grieving she'd have to endure.

That evening, Nadine joined Eliza and Tyler for their meal in the dining hall. They were halfway through their supper when Eliza spotted Royce heading their way with Ed Phillips at his side.

"Hello, my dear," Royce said to her with an artificial smile. "And who is your lovely friend?"

"This is Nadine," Eliza told him. "She's agreed to be my companion."

Royce's eyebrows lifted. Eliza could almost see his thoughts race over having the pretty young woman in their house. "How do you do, Miss…"

"Fitzgibbons," Nadine told him with that outrageous accent. "Of the Knob Hill Fitzgibbons. It's a pleasure to meet you, sir."

Eliza almost laughed out loud at the haughty-sounding name and voice. Nadine's proper name was plain old Morris. Eliza glanced at Tyler with unease, but he didn't know Nadine's last name, though he was obviously puzzled by her speech. He looked from her to Royce.

When Royce didn't acknowledge him, his expression fell, and he looked at his plate.

Eliza could have cheerfully stabbed Royce with her fork, but she twisted her napkin in her lap instead, wishing it was his neck. Before the month was over, he would be out of their lives forever, and she and her son would be establishing a new beginning. She would make it her purpose to see that her son felt wanted and important.

Royce wouldn't realize until too late that Eliza had packed and had her trunks taken to the train station. He would be furious. No doubt he would send Luther looking for her. Maybe even hire a Pinkerton. But she would cover their tracks and be long gone.

"This is Edward Phillips," Royce said to introduce the man. "He's the local banker. He keeps all my money safe."

Eliza couldn't help wondering how much money Royce had actually earned on his own. Hearing him claim as his own what her father had worked his whole life for set her teeth on edge.

"I've made an appointment for you at the dressmaker's," Royce told her. "And I took the liberty of asking Mrs. Grover to order special fabrics. I know you'll be pleased."

The fact that he'd done so and now told her in front of these people was humiliating. Eliza said nothing.

"The woman will be expecting you day after tomorrow."

He knew she wouldn't argue here. That's why he'd told her this way. She gave him a curt nod to acknowledge she'd heard him. She'd bet anything that among the fabrics were white satin and lace.

"He gives me the willies," Nadine said quietly, once the two men had moved to their own table.

"For good reason," Eliza told her in a tone so low that Tyler didn't hear. "I would never truly take you to that house and expose you to him."

"What about you?" Nadine asked, worry wrinkling her forehead.

"I'll be just fine," Eliza whispered. She was nowhere near fine. She was however, determined.

Eliza didn't see Jonas much during the next couple of days, and had the impression that he was avoiding her. On Thursday, once their morning chores were done, Eliza and Nadine headed out. Hattie Grover's shop was in her home on School Street, just past Second. It was a lovely morning, and the air smelled of lilacs, making Eliza supremely homesick. Two big bushes flanked the front porch at the Sutherland home and sent their fragrance all through the house on a day like this.

Hattie was a widow who'd done well by herself with her fine sewing. She had prepared tea and biscuits and arranged them on a silver tray. Her parlor was crowded because of the harpsichord wedged into the corner.

"Come sit for a spell," Hattie told them. "It's a treat for me to have guests. Oh, I know you're customers, but I need some feminine chatter from time to time."

"She's the customer," Nadine said with a laugh. "I'll be the guest and eat your fine rhubarb jam anytime."

They talked about the spring flowers and Hattie brought up an ice-cream social that the Ladies' Aid was holding the following month to raise money for new hymnbooks.

"That sounds like a right good time," Nadine told her.

"Look, we've finished all the tea," Hattie exclaimed. "You must be dry as a bone from all those biscuits. I'll go put the kettle on again." She scurried away.

"I'll never get a dress at this rate," Eliza said, not that she cared.

"Or fit into the ones you already have," Nadine added. They laughed.

Nadine got up and moved to the instrument in the corner. "Who plays this?" she called out. "Miss Hattie, may I play your harpsichord?" Then in a lower voice to Eliza, "I think this name on here is Italian."

She lifted the corner of a fringed scarf that hid the keys and touched a few of them, creating a melodious sound. "It has a very light touch."

"You know how to play?"

A crash from the direction of the kitchen arrested their attention. Nadine looked at Eliza with wide eyes.

"What was that?" Eliza called and stood. "Hattie, is everything all right?"

With Nadine on her heels, she dashed toward the back of the house, past the rooms where Hattie's dress mannequins and sewing supplies were kept, along a wallpapered hall to the kitchen.

The first thing to see was the kettle lying on the floor and a jar of cookies broken beside it. "Hattie?" Eliza called, not seeing the woman.

Nadine grabbed a length of toweling from a peg and knelt to mop up the water.

Eliza continued her search, pausing when she heard a sound coming from behind a closed paneled door. It sounded like a muffled voice.

"Hattie, is that you?" she called.

Nadine was right behind her, her hand on Eliza's arm.

"It must be the pantry door." Eliza grabbed the knob, turned and pushed the door open.

There, straight ahead of them lay Hattie, though a flour sack covered her face. Her hands and feet had been tied and she was lying on her side, squirming to get free. "What on earth?" Eliza said, hurrying forward to reach her.

A shuffling sounded beside her and Nadine slumped to the floor. Stunned, Eliza turned her head at the same time as a hand came around the front of her face and a foul-smelling cloth was pressed into her nose and mouth. She fought for breath.

Her last impressions were of a massive body behind her, a faint tobacco scent, and the steely grip on her upper body before the world swam out of focus and she lost consciousness.

Chapter Nineteen

Earlier, Quay had brought Jonas a supply order list. Jonas had read it over three times without really seeing anything before putting it aside and opening one of the ledgers. Finally, after he'd tallied a column four times with four different sums, he'd closed the book and pushed to his feet.

He tidied both desks, missing Eliza Jane's presence with a deep yearning. It went against his nature not to take control of a situation, not to head over to Dunlap's office and pound the tar out of him.

This time the fight was internal. A struggle to subdue himself and honor her wishes. He wouldn't do anything to hurt her or Tyler, and this was the way it had to be. He had to release them.

He opened a folder and studied the purchase contract for Eliza's shares of the brickyard. Her signature at the bottom was as basic and lovely as the woman herself. Now that he knew her…loved her, he didn't want to think about her leaving, about never seeing her again.

Everything was ready. They would take this over to the bank and make the transaction with a witness, just in time for her to catch her train. She predicted that Ed Phillips would alert Dunlap as soon as they walked from the building, and Jonas had no doubt she was correct.

But with everything sewn up legally, there was nothing the man could do. Except go after Eliza.

She would have to be long gone. Jonas might have to put a little pressure on Phillips to keep him from run ning straight to Dunlap until she had a good head start. He could manage that. Distract him. Hold him down if need be. Or, since Dunlap never actually did anything on his own, the thing to do would be to sit on Luther Vernon until she had a day or two's head start.

He liked that idea even better.

Just before noon, he roamed the kitchen, asking Lily what was on the menu. She made him a plate of fried chicken and creamy whipped potatoes and sent him out the door. "I'll send Yvonne with some rolls. We're short-handed back here without Nadine."

"Want me to hire you someone to fill in for a week or two?"

"I don't have time to train someone to work in my kitchen only a week or two. Only a man would conjure an idea like that."

He shrugged and carried his plate out to the dining room. The marshal had just seated himself, so Jonas took a spot beside him.

"That looks good," Warren said, eyeballing his plate.

Jonas set the prepared dinner in front of the marshal. "I'll get another one."

Lilibelle raised a brow and a spoon when he returned.

"I gave my lunch away. Set me up with another, will ya, please?"

She filled another plate and finally he sat to eat. He usually spotted Eliza Jane over the noon hour, but she was nowhere to be seen.

"Expecting someone?" Warren asked.

"Nope." Jonas bit unto a succulent crispy chicken leg.

"That Lilibelle can cook like nobody's business," the marshal said, wiping his chin.

Jonas nodded.

Yvonne brought them a basket of warm rolls. "Coffee for you both?"

"Thanks. Haven't seen Miss Sutherland this morning," Jonas said in what he hoped was a casual mention.

"Eliza Jane had an appointment with the dressmaker," Yvonne replied. "She told Ada she'd be back by noon."

"Nadine went with her?"

"I think so. I haven't seen either of them, anyway."

Eliza Jane didn't need to fill him in on her schedule. She'd been pretty standoffish since their last talk. Best they'd cooled things off before the break was permanent, he figured.

He and Warren were nearly finished with their meals when Ward stepped into the dining room doorway and glanced toward the back of the room. He spotted them and hurried to their table.

"We're almost done, but I'll sit with ya," Jonas offered.

"I came to give the marshal a message. Seems the preacher's wife took a pie over to Hattie Grover's and found her tied up in her pantry."

"Hattie Grover's the dressmaker, isn't she?" Jonas asked with a spark of alarm.

Warren nodded.

"Stella got Hattie calmed down," Ward continued. "And the two of them are at your office, waitin' for ya. Uriah went back to sit with them."

Jonas stood so fast his chair fell backward with a clatter.

Ward picked it up. "Calm down, Jonas."

Apprehension was already climbing Jonas's spine. "That's where Eliza Jane and Nadine went."

Both men grabbed their hats. Jonas ran ahead of Warren along Main Street to the marshal's office.

He'd never seen two people more out of place than Stella Miller and Hattie Grover. Amidst the clutter of the marshal's unkempt and dusty space, they perched on two chairs drawn close, frills at the cuffs and hems of their pastel dresses.

Uriah stood near a cloudy window, looking uncertain.

Hattie was trembling visibly.

"What happened?" Jonas asked.

Warren moved in beside him. "That's my job." He looked at the women. "What happened?"

"I had guests. Miss Sutherland and her little friend had joined me for tea."

"Miss Sutherland had a dress appointment," Stella

clarified, then aside to her friend asked, "Did you use the blue china pot?"

Hattie nodded.

"That's my favorite, too."

"Where are they now?" Jonas asked.

"Let her talk," Warren warned him.

Frustrated, Jonas moved back and settled a hip on the desk.

"I went back to put more water on the stove, and from out of nowhere someone grabbed me and pulled a flour sack over my head." Hattie patted her hair, as though her dignity and her hair had been mussed. "He was rough and very strong, so I know it was a man. He tied my feet and my wrists and dragged me into the pantry. I could tell it was the pantry, because I could smell the brine and the pickles."

"Hattie's pickles won a blue ribbon at the county fair last year," Stella remarked.

"What about Eliza Jane?" Jonas glared at Warren, impatient for him to get to the bottom of this.

"Then what happened?" Warren asked. "Do you know what happened to the other women?"

"They must have heard the commotion, because one of them called out. I think it was Miss Sutherland's voice. I heard footsteps as they ran back to the kitchen, and they called for me."

She sniffed and dabbed her nose with a lacy handkerchief. "The door to the pantry opened then. She said, 'What on earth,' just like that, and then there was a scuffle of some sort.

"I smelled a medicinal smell, quite unpleasant, and there was some thumping about and grunting, sounding as though someone was dragging something."

Jonas didn't like the sound of her story one bit. "Could you tell if this fella was dragging them outside?"

"That's what it sounded like. And after it got all quiet, I could tell the back door was open."

Stella verified that with a nod. "It was standing open when I got there."

"I thought I heard a wagon," Hattie mentioned. "There's a carriage house out back, but no one's used it since my husband passed. There is room for a wagon to pull back behind the house, though." She turned to her friend. "Did you see a wagon, Stella?"

The other woman shook her head. "I had left my pies cooling and was over at the church practicing on the organ. I wouldn't have heard a thing."

"What about the reverend?" the marshal asked. "Did he see anything?"

"He's out making calls around the county," Stella replied with a shake of her head. "Don't expect him till suppertime."

Warren nodded patiently. "We'll go have a look at your place, Mrs. Grover."

He turned to Jonas and they exchanged a look.

"Why don't the two of you go on over and let Bonnie fix you some tea?" Jonas suggested. Tea always made females feel better.

Their expressions brightened and the two women made their way out the door.

Once they were out of earshot, Jonas turned to Warren. "Same thing that happened to the boys."

The marshal turned to his young deputy. "Uriah, run down to the livery and saddle up our horses."

"Yes, sir!"

"Stop at the hotel," Jonas added. "Don't leave till you've asked everyone if they've seen Eliza Jane or Nadine."

Uriah nodded and shot out of the office.

They headed out and Jonas ran across the grassy lot to the west to look inside the schoolhouse. Children's heads turned and Miss Fletcher, who'd been writing on the blackboard, laid down the chalk.

"Everythin' good here today?" Jonas asked, keeping a light tone.

Tyler, seated at his desk, smiled and gave him a friendly wave.

"We're having a good day, thank you," the teacher replied.

Jonas ducked out and caught up with Warren, headed south. They crossed a brick street and came to the dressmaker's.

After a thorough check inside and out, they deduced that Hattie's account had been right. From the looks of it, someone had most likely hefted one woman over his shoulder and dragged the other out the back door and to a wagon that had been waiting behind a row of lilac bushes.

Even if Stella had looked out, she wouldn't have seen it, and the property to the south held only one house a quarter of a mile away. Beyond that, someone could've headed that wagon across open fields toward anywhere.

He had a bad feeling about this, but he couldn't let it influence his thinking. Could be they were back at the hotel, and all this fright was for nothing.

Uriah rode up leading their horses. "Nobody's seen 'em."

Jonas didn't like the fear that settled in his gut. All along he'd had his suspicions that Dunlap had something to do with Tyler's disappearance. It had all been too convenient. Dunlap had made a big show out of offering the reward and consoling her. He had assured Eliza Jane that he'd take care of everything.

"You two fall back while I look at these wagon tracks," he told Warren and Uriah.

Wheel tracks and droppings showed that a wagon with two horses had turned around and stopped for a spell. Then it had headed south on Second Street.

Jonas followed traces that led out of town and across a field. The marshal and his deputy followed.

A couple of miles from town, the tracks doubled back and led to a rocky gully that paralleled the foot-hills.

He signaled to the others. "I lost 'im here. No tellin' where he went. Could be anywhere."

"Go back for more men," Warren said to Uriah. "Get your bearings so you can tell 'em where to start lookin'."

Jonas pointed. "That's Bear Paw Ridge up there."

Uriah looked around, nodded and headed back at a gallop.

Jonas and Warren discussed where to meet to set up a camp if their search lasted into the night. They parted to look for signs of the women. Jonas rode until he had to stop to give his horse water.

The connection he couldn't prove or put his finger on ate at him. It was right there, but he couldn't see it. At that moment he felt as helpless as he had the night his mother had been killed. He wasn't having much more effect than a frightened, scrawny ten-year-old.

The black drank her fill at a clear water stream, and he let her graze in the nearby shade for a few minutes before continuing his search. Eventually darkness fell, as did his hopes for finding the women today. He made his way to the decided spot, where Silas and Warren were already cooking wild turkey eggs over a fire.

Several others joined them, including Curly Jack and Yale Baxter. Pool rode into the light of the campfire and slid from his horse. "Got somethin' you need t' see, Jonas."

Jonas got up and took the folded piece of paper.

You won't find her if I do not want you to. At ten o'clock tomorrow morning leave one thousand dollars cash in a saddlebag on a good horse. Tie the horse to the tree at the fork in the road that goes to Camas Creek and ride off. Come back the next day at the same time and your woman will be tied in the same place safe and sound. If you do not do what I say, you will not see her again.

The men had grown silent. Jonas read the note out loud.

"Is he talkin' about Miss Sutherland?" Warren asked.

Jonas nodded. Someone who knew he had feelings for Eliza Jane had written this.

"What about Nadine?" Curly Jack asked. "He only talked about one woman."

Uriah spoke up. "Maybe this fella wrote that note before he did anythin'. He coulda only figured on one female, but when they were together, he took 'em both."

"Where'd you get this?" Jonas asked Pool, holding up the note.

"Was tacked on the board outside my door," he answered. "Ever'body knows I run errands. If somebody wants a letter delivered or a chore done, they leave me a note."

Pool lived above the tailor's in a room with an outside stairway. No one would notice a person coming or going from his door because it was a normal event.

"Means he put the note there before he took the women and left town," Jonas said. "Uriah's right. Fella didn't expect Nadine to be along with Eliza Jane when she went to the dressmaker's."

"You gonna leave the money like he says?" Curly Jack asked.

Jonas folded the note and tucked it into his pocket. "If I don't find 'em first."

Chapter Twenty

Eliza's head throbbed, and her stomach felt queasy. She opened her eyes. In the dim light, cobwebs hung on a low wood plank ceiling. The walls were wood, too, chinked with dried mud.

She turned her head and spotted Nadine lying a few feet away, her hands and feet bound. Immediately, Eliza raised her wrists and stared at the strips of rawhide that tied them together. When she moved her legs, she discovered her ankles painfully bound.

"Nadine?" she called softly. "Nadine, are you all right?"

The other woman didn't respond. By using her body in a sideways inchworm motion, Eliza scooted until she was beside Nadine. "Nadine, wake up."

The young woman frowned, wrinkling her nose, but didn't open her eyes.

"Wake up!"

Nadine's eyelids fluttered. Gradually, she opened

her eyes and it took her a few minutes to focus on the ceiling. "Where are we?"

"I don't know. Does your head hurt?"

"Something awful."

"It's the chloroform."

"Somebody used chloroform on us?" Nadine rolled her head to look at Eliza. "Someone in Hattie's pantry? Or did I dream that part?"

"It was real. We went looking for her and got grabbed from behind. I heard and felt you go down beside me, and then my nose and mouth were covered."

"Why?"

Without an answer, Eliza managed to tuck her feet to the side, press her tied hands against the floor and rise to a sitting position. The room swam and her stomach lurched.

"Don't sit up too fast," she warned, closing her eyes against the kaleidoscope of swirling stars in the room.

"What does someone want with us?" Nadine asked, her eyes filled with fear. "I've heard terrible stories of women sold into slavery for bad things. I'd rather be dead than have that happen to me."

"I don't think that's going to happen," Eliza reassured her.

"How do you know?"

"Well. This is the same way Tyler and Ada's boys were taken. And they were returned. Maybe someone is trying to scare us. Or scare Jonas."

"It's working."

Eliza listened for sounds to tell her they were in

town or near town, but heard nothing. "When my head stops swimming, we'll see if we can get out of these bindings."

Eliza scooted to lean against a wall. She dozed, and when she woke, her head felt better, but her mouth and throat were parched. Squinting at the leather strips in the semidark didn't hurt her eyes so much now, so she drew her feet as close as she could and tried to work on the knots. From that position, it was impossible to get a good grasp on the ends.

Giving up, she scooted over to Nadine and started to work on her ankle bindings. Nadine woke and cried for a few minutes. "I thought the worst times of my life were behind me."

Eliza scooted so she could look her in the eye. "What do you think Jonas is doing right this minute?"

Nadine seemed to think for only a few seconds before she replied. "Looking for us."

"Exactly. Do you know anyone you'd rather have taking up for you?"

"No." She sniffled and brought her wrist up to dab at her nose.

"Well, there you go. Jonas is turning over every stone between Hattie's and—and wherever we are. He's going to find us."

"Okay."

"Meanwhile, let's help ourselves as much as we can. If we can get free, maybe we can make a run for it."

Nadine nodded her agreement.

Eliza wished she was as confident as she sounded.

She had no doubt that Jonas was looking for them. The marshal, too. She remembered the day they'd searched for Tyler. Looking didn't guarantee finding them, however, and she sure didn't have any confidence in their captor's mercy to keep them from harm.

She doubted they'd be able to simply open the door and waltz out once they were free, anyway, but she needed to do something.

Eliza's fingers were numb from the lack of circulation, making it all the more difficult to loosen Nadine's bindings. She worked at it for as long as she could, then paused and stretched her fingers awkwardly.

Nadine struggled to a sitting position and went to work on the ties at Eliza's wrists. Her fingers were much more nimble, and she got one knot loose and began on another. "Maybe all those sleight-of-hand card tricks were good for something."

"Good girl. Keep going."

They took turns like that, and after about an hour, Eliza's hands were freed. It felt so good, she extended and curled her fingers to get the blood flowing, then set to work on Nadine's bindings with renewed purpose.

A distant sound snagged her attention. As it grew louder, she recognized it as hoofbeats. An animal snorted and what sounded like feet hitting the ground and approaching the door alarmed her.

"Someone's here," Nadine whispered.

The door flew open and banged against the wall. The light hurt Eliza's eyes, and she threw her arm up over them instinctively.

"Well, well, what have we here?" The tall figure silhouetted against the daylight dropped a lumpy gunnysack on the floor. "Leaving so soon? Don't you like the accommodations?"

He kicked the door shut with one foot and stalked forward.

With the light gone, Eliza could see him. "Luther?"

He squatted and peered at her. "Are you surprised?"

"Did Royce put you up to this?"

He frowned as though she'd insulted him. "I'm sick of him calling the shots. Besides, what would he get outta having you snatched? All he wants is your Sutherland money and the business. If he'd put me up to anything, it would've been a bullet in your head. Then he'd have it all."

He had a point. So he'd done this on his own? "What do you want?"

"Your big shot intended is a cheap bastard. Five hundred dollars for the kid. You'd think his son would be worth more than that to him, wouldn't ya? The reward money didn't go very far, I can tell you that."

"Getting Tyler back meant everything to me," she told him. "Thank you for finding him."

He laughed. "It didn't take a whole lot of searchin', you twit. He was right here the whole time. I didn't have to find him. I left him here to start with."

"*You* kidnapped Tyler?"

"Now Royce *was* behind that one. He promised me the cash if I pulled it off so that it looked like his reward money had done the trick." He laughed. "I had everyone fooled."

Eliza stared at him, absorbing that information. Royce had paid this man to kidnap Tyler and then return him. "Why?"

"So he'd look like a hero, of course. His all-important money can make things happen. You were impressed, weren't you?"

She shook her head. No wonder Royce hadn't lifted a finger to look for Tyler or seemed the least concerned about the boy's welfare. He didn't care or he wouldn't have terrified the child like that, but he'd also planned his return.

"What do you want with us?" Nadine asked.

"I didn't plan on *you*," Luther said, turning to look at her. "I grabbed the Sutherland woman here, knowing Black would pay to get her back. But you were there, and I couldn't pass up the chance to double my profit. You're one of his little doves, aren't you?"

"Jonas Black is a decent man," Nadine said, bristling. "I have a respectable job."

He leaned forward to lift a length of Nadine's hair and twist it around his index finger. "Tomorrow morning, we'll find out if he thinks you're worth a thousand dollars. If he pays, then I'll tack another note to you. Asking double for *her*. Pretty smart, huh?"

"He'll pay," Nadine said. "He'll pay for both of us."

He sat back on his heels. "That's what we're all hopin', isn't it?"

He straightened and moved to the bag he'd left by the door. Reaching into it, he withdrew a crusty loaf of bread and a few apples. "This'll get you by." He placed the food on the floor near Eliza's knees. "Go ahead and eat."

Apparently he didn't care that her hands were untied. She reached to pick up the loaf and tore two pieces off, handing one to Nadine.

He moved away, took a seat on the floor near the opposite wall, and observed them as they slowly ate.

"Are you going to give us water?" Eliza asked sometime later. Her throat was dry and the taste of the chloroform lingered in her mouth.

He grimaced. "If I bring you water then I have to let you do your business."

"We drank a pot of tea this morning. We're going to have to do our business regardless," Nadine told him.

He took his time, going out and returning with a wooden bucket and ladle. Each of them drank their fill. He left the pail sitting where it was.

After rummaging through a dilapidated cupboard in a shadowy corner, he removed a dented kettle and set it beside Nadine with a clang. "You're not going out, so make do."

She and Eliza looked at each other.

"You'd best hope your lover shows up with the cash in the morning. If he does, your stay will be short."

"But we've seen you," Nadine said.

Eliza's heart sank. If he hadn't already thought of it, Nadine shouldn't have pointed out that they could identify him.

Chuckling, he knelt in front of her, took an apple and rubbed it on his pant leg. "Won't be the first time I've changed my name and started over. I'm sick of Royce, and I'm sick of your town. You won't see me again." He twisted off the stem and tossed it on the floor. "Don't worry your pretty head. You're worth more to me alive than dead. Besides, I only dispose of people when I'm paid to."

Eliza didn't know if the fact that he did kill for hire made her feel any better. But, he was right about them being worth more alive.

"Like your first lover," he said, taking a bite out of the fruit, squinting at Eliza and chewing loudly.

She looked at Nadine, then back at him. He'd been talking to her. "What?"

"Your first lover. Woods."

He'd confused her. "I don't know anyone named Woods."

"Not anymore, you don't. He's been under a pile of rocks out there on the ridge for years. I got a nice stash for that job. Enough to spend a year in Denver. That was part of the deal."

She remembered a time when she'd thought Luther was gone. That had been…years and events shifted in her memory. Woods?

Eliza felt as though she'd been pushed off a cliff. She couldn't catch her breath, and the ground was coming up to meet her fast. "Forest?" she croaked, past fear and revulsion.

Getting up, he laughed and threw the apple core toward the kettle. It hit it with a clang and bounced away into the dust. "Forest. Woods. That's the one."

"You killed Forest?" She could barely absorb the fact.

"Ah, hell, you're not gonna cry now, are ya? That musta been close to ten years ago."

The information swam in Eliza's head.

Leaning over, he touched Nadine's hair. She pulled away as far as she could.

He turned and left. A sliding sound followed the closing of the door. The horse nickered, then hoofbeats indicated his departure.

Forest hadn't run out on her. All the things he'd said and the promises he'd made had been true. Burning tears welled up and spilled over, and a sob broke from her throat.

He had loved her. He had truly wanted to marry her and be Tyler's father. He would have loved them and taken care of them. He would have been a loving father to her child. A child she could have kept and claimed to the entire world. She struck the floor with her fist, tears and emotions turning swiftly to anger. She'd known he was mercenary, but Royce had *killed* him. Paid that man to take Forest from her so he could have the coveted position beside her father.

"Are you all right?" Nadine asked, concerned but hesitating to get too close.

Eliza released a sound of supreme frustration and anger fired by grief. Grief for her. Grief for her son. Royce had robbed them. Robbed them and deliberately had a life taken for his own gain.

Poor Forest. She thought of him murdered and buried without family to mourn or a marker to save the place.

She dropped to lay in a huddle on the floor, and Nadine curved herself behind her, the best comfort she could manage.

Eventually, Eliza sat and took a shaky breath. "Let's eat apples."

After they each had one, she went straight to work on Nadine's wrist bindings. She picked and pulled until her fingertips were sore, but still she toiled at loosening the piece of leather.

Eventually, she got a spot free, then Nadine worked on it with her teeth while Eliza started on her ankles.

"I got it!" Nadine announced.

It was nearly dark. Eliza could barely see the other woman now. Nadine groped, brushed aside Eliza's hands and went back to the task.

Eliza awoke in pitch darkness to find her feet free. Her hips and shoulders ached from lying on the wood floor. She remembered Forest, and her chest ached with the loss. "Nadine?"

"Uh-huh."

"Are you loose?"

"Uh-huh. I tried the door. It doesn't budge. The wood covering the window, neither. What do you think this place is, anyway?"

"I don't know. Maybe a miner's old cabin."

"He might've left us a bed."

"Maybe it's best he didn't," Eliza pointed out. "It would likely have been home to mice or squirrels or some such."

"I do suppose we should count our blessings. What do we do now?"

"Wait for a little light, I guess. Maybe we can find some way out. Or something to use for a weapon."

"Do you think he's still looking for us?" Nadine asked, her voice sounding childlike in the darkness.

"I expect he's lying awake, waiting for first light so he can find us," Eliza replied.

"Yes," the other girl assured herself. "That's it exactly."

Chapter Twenty-One

Jonas saddled the black in the semidarkness, tied on his full canteen and pulled himself onto the animal's back with a groan. He'd become soft from sleeping in his feather bed for the past few years. It seemed a lifetime ago that he'd slept on the ground for weeks, even months at a time.

The others were rising around the camp. He hadn't missed the sound of men's early-morning hacking and grumping. "I'm headin' out," he called.

"We'll meet here at nine," Warren called. "If no one's had any luck finding them, we'll wait here while Jonas delivers the money."

"Pool, you take that note I gave you to Ward and tell him to put a thousand dollars in a bag and send it with you. Don't be late. That money is what this man wants. Lives will depend on it."

"Yessir, Jonas. I'll do it just like you said."

Jonas prodded the horse into motion.

By the time it was light enough to see he'd made his way back to where he'd left off searching the night before. Dew glistened on grass and weeds, and the sound of birds made it seem like a normal day. The horse startled a chicken hawk, and it flapped its way up into the air and across the bright blue sky.

He was letting them down. Gritting his teeth, he studied the surrounding trees and woodlands. Eliza Jane and Nadine needed him, and he was blindly combing the mountainside.

Hope had run out by the time he checked his pocket watch. He headed back to the campsite. Whiskered faces were glum as Pool held out the saddlebag. Jonas looked at the money, then strapped the bag to the horse Pool had brought and headed for the designated spot.

The kidnapper had chosen the perfect spot. This place was easily visible for half a mile in three directions. Even if he was fool enough to go against the demands in the ransom note, there was no place to hide and watch.

The women's captor was probably up in the hills to the southeast, watching him leave the horse and money.

After tying the bay to the tree, he patted its neck, mounted and rode away.

Jonas was mad now. Mad enough to pound the tar out of somebody. Mad enough to ride back to town.

The brickyard sat at the southeast corner of Silver Bend, and Sutherland land took up a couple of acres. Approaching from the rear, he crossed railroad tracks and passed wood-constructed drying sheds. To the east were tiny hutlike buildings where employees and their families ate and slept. He reached the ramps that led up to another wooden building, where workers were shoveling clay onto conveyor belts.

As Jonas neared Third Street, the brick buildings and tree-lined drive looked like a different place. An ornamental brass plaque on the lush front lawn proclaimed Sutherland Brick Company.

Jonas tethered his horse to a hitching post and strode inside.

A man with neatly parted and combed hair sat at the desk in a large carpeted foyer. "How may I help you, sir?" he asked.

"I wanna see Dunlap."

"Do you have an appointment?"

"Where is he?"

"What's your name?"

"Black."

Giving Jonas a wary look, the bespectacled man got up and walked through a doorway.

Jonas cut around the desk and followed. The man rapped on a door with a panel of frosted glass. Dunlap's name had been lettered in fancy script. Jonas pushed past him and entered the office.

"Here, now, you can't—"

"Nice place, Dunlap," Jonas said, looking around.

Royce, who'd been seated at a large mahogany desk, got to his feet. "What are you doing here?"

"You've got some talkin' to do."

Royce waved the other man away, and he backed out

of the room, closing the door. "You must be referring to my fiancée. I just heard the news."

Jonas strode to the corner of Royce's desk. "Don't play dumb. Your little plot won't work this time."

"What do you mean?"

"I know you had somethin' to do with Tyler's disappearance."

Royce moved to the opposite corner, putting the entire desk between them. "You can't prove that."

Jonas lunged across, missing Royce when he dodged, but catching him as he tried to make a run for the door. He hauled him back by his fancy coat and pressed him backward on the glossy wood surface. Papers fluttered and a stack of folders slid into a jumble on the floor.

With Royce's collar in his fist, he held the man captive and leaned over him. "Maybe I can't prove it yet, but I will. If you've done something to Eliza Jane, I'm gonna smear you from here to your fancy front lawn."

Royce's face turned red from exertion and lack of air. "It wasn't me," he gasped. "And who'll go to jail for that? You're the hothead and everybody knows it."

"I want to know where she is," Jonas said through gritted teeth.

"I don't know. You can kill me, and I still can't tell you. Why would I kidnap my own fiancée?"

Jonas wanted to choke him senseless. "For the same reason you do everything. Money."

"What money?"

"The thousand dollars I left out at the fork to Camas Creek half an hour ago for starters?"

"You paid ransom?"

"Of course I paid it."

Royce's eyes widened. "That son of a—"

"Who? Who has her?"

Royce struggled, but Jonas was stronger.

Jonas tightened his grip on the other man's throat. "This is your last chance to tell me." He drew a knife from his pocket and flipped it open.

Royce's eyes bulged white in his red face.

Jonas brought the blade up under Royce's chin and pricked his skin.

Dunlap cursed without much force since he had no air. "Pro-bably Lu-ther," he managed.

Jonas relaxed his grip just enough to let him speak. "Your pal, Vernon? Where is he?"

"I don't know."

"Where is he?"

Royce coughed.

"Where did he hold Tyler?" Jonas demanded and poked the blade of the knife against Dunlap's flesh.

Royce knew Jonas wasn't letting up. "Release me and I'll tell you."

Disgusted, Jonas let go.

Gasping, Royce turned to one side and loosened his collar.

"Where?" Jonas barked.

"He told me there was a miner's cabin due north of that fork in the trail. He said you can see Bear Paw Ridge from the front of the cabin."

Jonas backed away and flipped the knife closed. "If she's hurt in any way, you're answerin' to me."

He stalked from the room.

Royce got to his feet in a rage. If Jonas got to Luther, the idiot would tell everything. Holding his neck, he yanked open a drawer and took out a gun.

Chapter Twenty-Two

Jonas barely paused at the campsite, shouting the location to Warren and Pool, then pushed the black as hard as he dared. Nearing the general location, he studied the ground. Within minutes, Jonas spotted horse droppings.

He followed trampled weeds near the crest of a hill. Dismounting and hobbling the horse, he grabbed his rifle and walked nearly to the top then crawled the rest of the way. Outlining himself against the sky on a hilltop wasn't smart if anyone was on the other side.

In the valley below, a wagon sat beside a rustic cabin. There was no sign of life, no livestock of any kind and no smoke rising from the stone chimney. By all appearances the place had been abandoned for some time. But the wagon was a giveaway.

He checked the chamber in his rifle, then watched the cabin and surrounding woods for a long time. He was about to go down and investigate when the sound of falling rocks caught his attention.

From the north, a rider made his circuitous way down the hillside, following a deer trail probably, and rode out into the open toward the cabin. Following on a tether was the bay Jonas had tied to the tree. Sure enough, the bag was draped across Vernon's saddle.

Riding down on him now would only put the women in danger. Jonas contemplated his next move. Warren and more men would be moving in soon. But once Luther got inside, anything could happen.

Jonas took careful aim. He could pick him off easily from here. He wasn't a murderer, though, so he focused on putting the bullet in Luther's shoulder. Right there.

A shot rang out, and the bullet hit the corner of the cabin. Jonas lowered the barrel, searching for where the shot had come from.

How the hell had Dunlap gotten so close without Jonas hearing him? Royce slid from a horse and ran behind a stack of firewood.

Luther jumped from the horse and walked beside it using the animal as a shield, then shoved aside a bar on the cabin door. Apparently not taking any chances on losing his means of escape, he must have tethered or hobbled the lead horse because it didn't move away from the front of the cabin.

"What are you doing?" Royce shouted.

Luther ducked inside, but his head and shoulders appeared around the doorway. "I'm making up for your lousy pay."

"You idiot, you're making a mess of everything!" Royce shouted.

"So you're going to kill me yourself?" Luther returned. "I didn't know you had it in you."

Royce fired, the shot hitting a wood shingle and sending it sailing.

Luther laughed uproariously and returned fire, nicking a log and sending Royce scrambling. "I hope you brought reinforcements!"

"You can't stay in there forever," Royce called.

"And you can't last a night out there," Luther returned. "There's bears and snakes in those woods, you know."

Royce looked behind him, and then caught himself.

The grass rustled behind and below Jonas, and he turned to discover Warren and several of the other men silently making their way up the hillside. They must have heard the shots.

Warren signaled for quiet and came up beside Jonas.

Jonas ducked down to talk to him. "Vernon has the women inside, I'm sure. Dunlap rode in and shot at 'im. I missed a good shot myself when he did that."

The marshal watched the exchange between the two men for a moment. "We couldn't get lucky and one of them shoot the other."

"Dunlap couldn't hit the side of a barn if you helped 'im aim."

"Those are the scariest ones," Warren remarked.

Another shot rang out.

"Let's try to get someone to surrender." The marshal crawled to a better position behind a rock. Leaning around it, he called, "We've got you surrounded! Lay down your guns and we won't shoot."

"Look there, you stupid fool, you've involved the law," Royce shouted.

"If you want these woman alive, ride out!" Luther called.

"You can't get past us," Warren returned. "Send them out, and we won't shoot you."

"How about you let me get on my horse and give me a head start?" Luther called. "And do something about that idiot Royce! Then I'll let them go."

Warren looked at Jonas and Jonas nodded. They could ride him down once the women were safe.

"Okay!" Warren called. He turned to Uriah. "Go get Dunlap's gun."

Uriah worked his way down the hill.

"Our guns are on you, Dunlap," Warren called. "Give up the .45."

Infuriated, Royce studied the hill behind him, his gaze flickering back to the doorway, and finally he tossed the revolver onto the ground.

Uriah scrambled out of the brush and picked it up.

"Get on your horse!" the marshal called to Luther.

"Don't follow me, or I'll turn around and shoot your ladies."

"All right!" Warren called.

The door closed. It seemed an eternity before it opened again and Luther came out with Eliza Jane in front of him, his arm across her neck, and Nadine following. Both women's hands were tied, and it looked as though they were bound together at the waist, as well.

"Let my fiancée go," Royce called.

"Shut the hell up," Jonas said softly, alerted to worse trouble.

"Don't you worry, my dear. I'll take care of this." Royce moved out from behind the woodpile and approached Luther as he neared the horses.

"Stay back!" Jonas called.

Eliza Jane's gaze shot to Jonas at the top of the hill.

"Get back," Luther told him. "You don't give two bits about this woman, and you're not fooling anybody."

Royce raised the barrel of a gun.

"Where'd he get that?" Warren asked.

Royce fired.

All movement happened at once after that.

Nadine slumped to the ground, a red stain spreading across her chest.

The rope tying her to Eliza tightened, pulling Eliza down with her.

Vulnerable now, Luther raised his gun and shot Royce, then made a dash for the horses.

Royce fell back spread-eagle in the dust.

Jonas was over the top of the hill and down to the clearing in seconds, as Warren and others ran for their horses to follow Luther.

Jonas kept his rifle aimed at Royce as he ran past. The man wasn't dead yet, but his eyes were twitching and blood rolled from the corner of his mouth.

Eliza Jane was on her knees. She'd wadded up her skirt hem and pressed it to the wound in Nadine's shoulder.

Seeing that Eliza was all right, Jonas took the material

from her and held it away to look at the bullet hole under Nadine's collarbone. "It's your shoulder," he said to her. "We'll get you to Doc's and you'll be okay."

She gave him a weak smile, though he knew how badly she was hurting. "Eliza Jane said you'd come for us."

Jonas took a pocketknife from his hip pocket and sliced the rope at her wrists. He then removed Eliza Jane's bindings and held both of her hands. "Did he hurt you?"

Eliza Jane shook her head, pulled her hands free and reached for him.

Nothing had ever felt as good as her breasts crushed to him and her arms around his waist. He buried his face in her hair and gave his heart permission to beat again. If anything had happened to her…if he'd lost her… He couldn't bear to think of it.

"Is Tyler all right?" she asked against his chest.

"Ada's takin' care of him. He's fine."

Pool and Yale showed up. "We've got horses hooked to that wagon. Let's get Miss Nadine in the bed careful-like."

Eliza pulled away from Jonas so he could rise and help them. She turned to look at Royce where he lay motionless. Getting to her feet, she got up and walked toward him.

Eliza couldn't make herself kneel at his side. She stood over him. She'd been present at the deaths of both her parents and her sister, and the memories of her pain in those moments were vivid.

Looking at Royce, watching the life drain from

him, she felt nothing. He'd carved away any bit of caring or sympathy she could ever have felt where he was concerned.

"Well, *my dear,*" she said, wondering why she bothered, but unable to stop herself. "Just so you know, I wasn't planning to stick around. I was leaving. And I sold my shares of the company to finance my trip."

Something flickered in his eyes, and he struggled to bring her into focus.

"Yes," she continued. "Your new partner would have been Jonas Black. I almost regretted not being around to witness your reaction. But now I will be around. And let's see, your shares will go to my father's next of kin. I guess that would be…me."

He blinked and tried to speak, but only coughed up more blood.

Jonas walked up beside her.

"I know you had Forest killed," she said.

Royce blinked again.

Jonas looked from her to Royce.

"Jonas isn't really interested in running the brick-yard," she continued. "I did a good job of it before, so I guess I'll handle it until Tyler's old enough. I'll make investments and improvements and turn a handsome profit. I'll spend money on the workers' quarters. Jonas can help there."

She turned and looked at the man she spoke of. "Jonas is a good man. The best man I've ever known. In fact… I'm going to ask him to marry me." She reached for Jonas's hand and looked back down at Royce. "And if he says yes, we'll have children. More sons I hope. And you…you will be dead."

Jonas put his other hand on her shoulder. "You ready? The men will take him now."

She turned away. "Luther said there's a pile of stones up on that ridge somewhere. That's where he buried Forest."

Jonas met her gaze with sympathy.

"Royce paid Luther to kill him. He didn't leave me. He loved me, just like he said."

Love shone from the look he gave her. "Of course he did."

Eliza didn't turn back around. "That man can't ruin any more of my life. He stole everything from me. Everything. The man I loved. My child."

He glanced beyond her. "He can't steal anything anymore, Eliza Jane."

She closed her eyes and tears escaped anyway. She brought her hands up to cover her face. As much as she hated the weakness, she cried. "I'm free. I'm finally free."

"You've suffered enough," he told her. "Can't let the past get in the way of your future. I know what I'm talkin' about."

She took the hand he offered, and he led her up the hillside. They searched for half an hour, until the men in the clearing below were gone and the birds sang again.

And finally Jonas cleared the brush away from a pile of stones. A pile that wasn't a natural slide, but a deliberate grouping about the length of a man.

Jonas removed his hat.

Eliza knelt by the weathered rocks. "I'm so glad I know the truth," she said softly. "I'm so sad you died like this. I'm sorry. And I'm sorry I didn't believe in you."

Jonas swallowed hard and raised his face to the sunlight. Any man would be lucky to have this woman love him.

After a few minutes of silence, she stood and turned to him. "I'm ready. Let's go home."

Jonas led her down to the clearing where he'd left his horse and handed her his canteen. "Where's home gonna be?" he asked.

Her gaze touched the hillside, then his face. She took a drink and handed back the canteen. "I have a perfectly good home that my father built from bricks from the first kiln. Of course I'd need a husband to live there with me."

"Will I do?"

"Will you marry me?"

Jonas hung the canteen on the saddle horn and took off his hat. "Tried askin' you that a hundred times."

"A hundred and one might be the one."

He took her hand and kissed her fingers, laid his palm along her dirty cheek. "I love you with a love so fierce and strong I can hardly stand it sometimes. When I believed I had to let you go, I thought I'd never take a deep breath again or sleep a night without achin' for you.

"Marry me and I'll never let you go. I'll love you and Tyler, and be a good father t' the boy."

Eliza placed her hand on his cheek and her other arm around his neck, drawing him to her for a kiss she hoped showed him he held her heart and she trusted him with it.

The sun warmed their heads and shoulders, and their hearts beat in a rhythm as ancient as the mountains that towered above them.

"I'll marry you," Eliza told him on a sigh. "A woman never knows when she might need a hero."

* * * * *

Silhouette Desire kicks off 2009 with
MAN OF THE MONTH,
*a yearlong program featuring incredible heroes
by stellar authors.*

When navy SEAL Hunter Cabot returns home for
some much-needed R and R, he discovers he's a
married man. There's just one problem: he's never
met his "bride."

*Enjoy this sneak peek at Maureen Child's
AN OFFICER AND A MILLIONAIRE.
Available January 2009 from Silhouette Desire.*

One

Hunter Cabot, Navy SEAL, had a healing bullet wound in his side, thirty days' leave and, apparently, a wife he'd never met.

On the drive into his hometown of Springville, California, he stopped for gas at Charlie Evans's service station. That's where the trouble started.

"Hunter! Man, it's good to see you! Margie didn't tell us you were coming home."

"Margie?" Hunter leaned back against the front fender of his black pickup truck and winced as his side gave a small twinge of pain. Silently then, he watched as the man he'd known since high school filled his tank.

Charlie grinned, shook his head and pumped gas. "Guess your wife was lookin' for a little 'alone' time with you, huh?"

"My—" Hunter couldn't even say the word. *Wife?* He didn't have a wife. "Look, Charlie..."

"Don't blame her, of course," his friend said with a wink as he finished up and put the gas cap back on.

"You being gone all the time with the SEALs must be hard on the ol' love life."

He'd never had any complaints, Hunter thought, frowning at the man still talking a mile a minute. "What're you—"

"Bet Margie's anxious to see you. She told us all about that R and R trip you two took to Bali." Charlie's dark brown eyebrows lifted and wiggled.

"Charlie..."

"Hey, it's okay, you don't have to say a thing, man."

What the hell could he say? Hunter shook his head, paid for his gas and as he left, told himself Charlie was just losing it. Maybe the guy had been smelling gas fumes too long.

But as it turned out, it wasn't just Charlie. Stopped at a red light on Main Street, Hunter glanced out his window to smile at Mrs. Harker, his second-grade teacher who was now at least a hundred years old. In the middle of the crosswalk, the old lady stopped and shouted, "Hunter Cabot, you've got yourself a wonderful wife. I hope you appreciate her."

Scowling now, he only nodded at the old woman—the only teacher who'd ever scared the crap out of him. What the hell was going on here? Was everyone but him nuts?

His temper beginning to boil, he put up with a few more comments about his "wife" on the drive through town before finally pulling into the wide, circular drive leading to the Cabot mansion. Hunter didn't have a clue what was going on, but he planned to get to the bottom of it. Fast.

He grabbed his duffel bag, stalked into the house and paid no attention to the housekeeper, who ran at him, fluttering both hands. "Mr. Hunter!"

"Sorry, Sophie," he called out over his shoulder as he took the stairs two at a time. "Need a shower, then we'll talk."

He marched down the long, carpeted hallway to the rooms that were always kept ready for him. In his suite, Hunter tossed the duffel down and stopped dead. The shower in his bathroom was running. His *wife?*

Anger and curiosity boiled in his gut, creating a churning mass that had him moving forward without even thinking about it. He opened the bathroom door to a wall of steam and the sound of a woman singing— off-key. Margie, no doubt.

Well, if she was his wife...Hunter walked across the room, yanked the shower door open and stared in at a curvy, naked, temptingly wet woman.

She whirled to face him, slapping her arms across her naked body while she gave a short, terrified scream.

Hunter smiled. "Hi, honey. I'm home."

* * * * *

Be sure to look for
AN OFFICER AND A MILLIONAIRE
by USA TODAY bestselling author
Maureen Child.
Available January 2009 from Silhouette Desire.

CELEBRATE
60 YEARS
OF PURE READING PLEASURE
WITH **HARLEQUIN**®!

We'll be spotlighting a different series
every month throughout 2009
to celebrate our 60th anniversary.
Look for Silhouette Desire® in January!

MAN of the MONTH

Collect all 12 books in the Silhouette Desire®
Man of the Month continuity, starting in
January 2009 with *An Officer and a Millionaire*
by *USA TODAY* bestselling author
Maureen Child.

*Look for one new Man of the Month title
every month in 2009!*

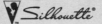

REQUEST YOUR FREE BOOKS!

Harlequin® Historical
Historical Romantic Adventure!

2 FREE NOVELS PLUS 2 FREE GIFTS!

YES! Please send me 2 FREE Harlequin® Historical novels and my 2 FREE gifts (gifts are worth about $10). After receiving them, if I don't wish to receive any more books, I can return the shipping statement marked "cancel". If I don't cancel, I will receive 6 brand-new novels every month and be billed just $4.94 per book in the U.S. or $5.49 per book in Canada, plus 25¢ shipping and handling per book and applicable taxes, if any*. That's a savings of 20% off the cover price! I understand that accepting the 2 free books and gifts places me under no obligation to buy anything. I can always return a shipment and cancel at any time. Even if I never buy another book, the two free books and gifts are mine to keep forever.

246 HDN ERUM 349 HDN ERUA

Name _____ (PLEASE PRINT) _____

Address _____ Apt. # _____

City _____ State/Prov. _____ Zip/Postal Code _____

Signature (if under 18, a parent or guardian must sign)

Mail to the **Harlequin Reader Service:**
IN U.S.A.: P.O. Box 1867, Buffalo, NY 14240-1867
IN CANADA: P.O. Box 609, Fort Erie, Ontario L2A 5X3

Not valid to current subscribers of Harlequin Historical books.

Want to try two free books from another line?
Call 1-800-873-8635 or visit www.morefreebooks.com.

* Terms and prices subject to change without notice. N.Y. residents add applicable sales tax. Canadian residents will be charged applicable provincial taxes and GST. Offer not valid in Quebec. This offer is limited to one order per household. All orders subject to approval. Credit or debit balances in a customer's account(s) may be offset by any other outstanding balance owed by or to the customer. Please allow 4 to 6 weeks for delivery. Offer available while quantities last.

Your Privacy: Harlequin Books is committed to protecting your privacy. Our Privacy Policy is available online at www.eHarlequin.com or upon request from the Reader Service. From time to time we make our lists of customers available to reputable third parties who may have a product or service of interest to you. If you would prefer we not share your name and address, please check here. ☐

HH08R

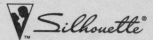

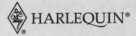

HARLEQUIN®

American ★ Romance®

TINA LEONARD
The Texas
Ranger's Twins

Men Made in America

The promise of a million dollars has lured
Texas Ranger Dane Morgan back to his family
ranch. But he can't be forced into marriage to
single mother of twin girls, Suzy Wintertone,
who is tempting as she is sweet—can he?

Available January 2009
wherever books are sold.

LOVE, HOME & HAPPINESS

COMING NEXT MONTH FROM

HARLEQUIN®
HISTORICAL

- **TEXAS RANGER, RUNAWAY HEIRESS**
  by **Carol Finch**
  (Western)
  Texas Ranger Hudson Stone can't disobey orders. He must find Gabrielle Price. Hud believes her to be a spoiled, self-centered debutante—but discovers she's more than capable of handling herself in adversity! Bri enflames his desires—but the wealthy, forbidden beauty is strictly off-limits!

- **MARRYING THE CAPTAIN**
  by **Carla Kelly**
  (Regency)
  Oliver Worthy, a captain in the Channel Fleet, is a confirmed bachelor—so falling in love with Eleanor Massie is about the last thing he intended! Eleanor loves Oliver, too, although her humble past troubles her. But in the turbulence of a national emergency, Eleanor will fight to keep her captain safe....

- **THE VISCOUNT CLAIMS HIS BRIDE**
  by **Bronwyn Scott**
  (Regency)
  For years, Valerian Inglemoore lived a double life on the war-torn Continent. Now he's returned, knowing exactly what he wants—Philippa Stratten, the woman he gave up for the sake of her family.... But Philippa is not the hurt, naive debutante he once knew and is suspicious of his intentions....

- **HIGH SEAS STOWAWAY**
  by **Amanda McCabe**
  (Renaissance)
  Meeting Balthazar Grattiano years after their first fateful encounter, Bianca Simonetti finds he is no longer the spoiled, angry young nobleman she knew. Now he has sailed the seas, battled pirates and is captain of his own ship. Bianca is shocked to find her old infatuation has deepened to an irresistible sexual attraction....